SEAL'S DELIVERANCE

TAKE NO PRISONERS

BOOK #9

ELLE JAMES

New York Times & USA Today
Bestselling Author

Dedication

This book is dedicated to:

My daughters who have followed in their mama's bootsteps and joined the military.

My wonderful buddy, Nora, who got me to join the USAF and led me to some wonderful friendships I value dearly.

My most voracious readers who wait so patiently for my next book release!

Elle's Belles and Myla's Mavens who help me get the word out when I have a new release, as well as helping me make decisions about what's next. You guys are great.

I love you all so much!

Escape with...
Elle James
aka Myla Jackson

Author's Note

Visit **ellejames.com** for more
titles and release dates

Also visit her alter-ego Myla Jackson at
mylajackson.com

About This Book

Navy SEAL and a sexy CDC biologist join forces in Montana to find the one responsible for threatening revenge on the SEAL team's loved ones through biological terrorism

Raymond "Sting Ray" Thompson returns home to Eagle Rock, Montana, when a trail of treachery leads him back with members of his SEAL team. Their mission: to locate the biological terrorist targeting people closest to them. Claiming retribution for destroying an Ethiopian factory generating a deadly virus, the terrorist strikes Sting Ray's uncle, the man who raised him. His team joins forces with a group of former military men to ferret out the terrorist and halt the release of the deadly virus into the environment.

On vacation from her job with the CDC, Lilly Parker is with her brother in Montana when she gets the call to investigate a potential biological disaster targeting a family member of a Navy SEAL. Working with the Brotherhood Protectors and a team of Navy SEALs, Lilly conducts a covert investigation. Lilly and Sting Ray join forces to trace the virus to its source, determined to contain the disaster and protect the community, while fighting their mutual attraction.

Chapter One

Ray Thompson—Sting Ray to his teammates—slowed as he neared the apartment complex in Little Creek, Virginia where he kept the few belongings he'd acquired since he'd joined SEAL Team 10 four years previously. He glanced at the complex, each entrance exactly the same as the others, every apartment the same size and shape, only differentiated by what the occupants brought to furnish the interiors.

None of his belongings were worth much. He'd picked them up in thrift stores or the nearby warehouse-style superstore. None of it mattered. Nothing made it feel like a home. The apartment served only one purpose—it was a place to park his gear between assignments.

If he had to transfer to another base, he would call the local women's shelter and have them pick up the microfiber futon, mattress, boxed springs and flat screen television he watched the Denver Broncos on when he was in town during football season. Yeah, it wasn't much, but he liked it that way. He'd never really felt like his uncle's place was home—no warmth, no deep affection, no reason to return—and it made it easier when he got orders to ship out.

Home. Since getting back from his fifth deployment in as many months, this last one to the sands of Riyadh, Saudi Arabia, he'd been thinking more about home. His teammates were all falling in love and settling into their lives with their women. The Friday nights of bar-hopping and Sunday beer, pizza and football were less and less frequent and now included females in the once all-male group dynamic.

Sting Ray couldn't begrudge his battle buddies their newfound happiness. Some men found the women of their dreams. And his teammates had found some beautiful women who were as strong and just as dedicated to making the world a better place as SEAL Team 10. But he thought he'd fallen down that rabbit hole called love once, got burned and had the scars to prove it.

No thanks. He liked being single. He didn't have to check with his woman to know whether he could go out for a beer or watch the game on his own television. Now, sex was another thing entirely. Although he'd given up on relationships, he hadn't given up on nature's best form of stress relief. He just hadn't met anyone lately who tempted him.

Looking back, he wasn't sure he'd been committed to any relationship. If he was fair to his ex-girlfriend, he had to admit to being distant and non-communicative. He blamed that on his uncle. The man had rarely talked.

Before girlfriends, one or two of his teammates who lived in the same apartment complex would run with him. Lately, they preferred to exercise in bed into the late mornings on weekends. Especially since they'd returned from their latest assignment at a Saudi Arabian prince's palace in Riyadh. They'd helped the prince dodge a major biological warfare bullet aimed at the royal family.

The four-man team had secretly made it in, and come out relatively unscathed, having located the vial of toxic virus before it could be unleashed on anyone.

A lot of African villagers hadn't been so lucky. The biological weapon of mass destruction had been tested on entire isolated villages in Somalia and Ethiopia. Not a solitary soul lived to tell who had done it or how. Fortunately, their search had uncovered the manufacturing source and shut it down. But not before several vials had made their way out of the facility.

Sting Ray stretched and stared around the neighborhood of tightly-packed houses and apartment complexes. He'd personally witnessed the horrible devastation to one small, African village. He couldn't imagine the destruction that would occur, if one of those vials were unleashed in Little Creek, Virginia.

Back on American soil, he could almost forget such dangers existed. But there was always another bad guy to stop. And he'd be ready for it, mentally and physically. He wondered what their next assignment might be. Having run five miles that morning, he still had to shower and change into his uniform before he reported to the Naval

Base and his team that morning.

Tires screeched behind him.

About to step off the sidewalk and into the parking lot of the apartment building, Sting Ray stepped back in time to keep from walking into a black, crew-cab, four-by-four pickup barreling to a stop in front of him.

He jumped back and yelled, "God damn you, Irish! You almost ran over me."

Irish, one of his teammates, stuck his head out of the window, his face grim. "Get in," he said, jerking his head toward the back door. "We have serious trouble."

The grim expression on his teammate's face washed Sting Ray's anger away in an instant. He flung open the back door, slid in and nodded to Ben "Big Bird" Sjodin, who filled the front seat, wearing an old North Dakota Fighting Sioux T-shirt and jogging shorts.

"What's up?" Sting Ray asked, his deployment meter on high-alert. "Are we shipping out?"

Irish nodded. "Looks like it." He glanced in the rearview mirror. "Have you checked your phone or text messages in the last fifteen minutes?"

Sting Ray frowned and glanced at the cell phone strapped to his arm. Yeah, he'd felt it vibrate a minute or two ago, but he'd been so close to his apartment complex he hadn't bothered to stop and check the message, figuring his boss or teammates would text twice in a row if it had been an actual emergency. Or better still, they would have set off his phone finder alarm and blasted his eardrums. "I haven't. Why? Did I miss anything?"

Big Bird turned in his seat to look back at Sting Ray. "You might have. I'd check it if I were you."

Sting Ray pulled the phone from the strap on his arm, entered his screen lock password and brought up his text messages. At the top of the messages was a text from an unknown number. He opened the text and read, a chill creeping across his sweat-soaked skin.

You took something of value from me
Now, I will take something of value from you
Someone you care about

Sting Ray glanced up, his gaze connecting with Big Bird's. "You know about this?"

Big Bird nodded. "I got one just like it. I called Yasmin immediately. She's on her way to meet us at Irish's apartment. Claire's there."

"We were at the gym when we got the texts," Irish said. "Claire got a text as well."

"Have you checked with anyone else on the team?" Sting Ray read the message again, his gut clenching.

"Only the three of us and Claire got the text." Irish whipped out of the parking lot and back onto the road. "Tuck is concerned. He wants us to meet him at the war room on base."

"Who would send something out like that?" Sting Ray asked. "And how did they get all of our numbers?"

"Dude, what do the four of us have in common?" Big Bird asked, his gaze narrowing.

"We were all in Ethiopia when we stormed the biological weapons factory," Sting Ray said. His eyes widened. "Damn."

"Yeah. Damn." Irish shot a glance in the rearview mirror. "As soon as I got the message, I called Claire. So far, she's okay, but I'm worried about her. If whoever was involved in the manufacturing of the biological weapons has access to some of the virus they were producing, we could be in a lot of trouble."

"Along with the people we care most about," Big Bird added. "Now that we know it's just those who were responsible for destroying the lab, we know who's targeted."

"We know who they want to hurt, but we don't know who they'll hurt that we might care about," Sting Ray said. "You're assuming it will be your women."

Irish and Big Bird both nodded.

"Neither of us have family left," Irish said. "Other than the other members of SEAL Team 10, all we have are our women."

"What about you?" Big Bird asked. "You've never mentioned any family that I know of."

"And you don't have a woman," Irish added.

Sting Ray snorted. "Thanks for the reminder. You're making me sound pathetic."

"No, actually, you're lucky." Irish's brows dipped. "I'm worried about Claire. She's not a trained warrior. She's a doctor. She's vulnerable."

"At least, Yasmin knows not to trust anyone and she's trained to take care of herself." Big Bird's fists bunched. "But against an unknown force, she'll be at risk, as well."

"So, do you have someone you're close to?" Irish asked.

An image of a grizzled mountain man flashed in Sting Ray's mind. "The only person I have left that I can call family is my Uncle Fred."

"Uncle Fred?" Big Bird frowned. "I don't remember you ever talking about him."

"Wait." Irish looked at him in the rearview mirror. "Is he the man you go hunting with every fall when we're not on a mission?"

Sting Ray nodded.

"Doesn't he live in Montana, or somewhere up that direction?"

Again, Sting Ray nodded and a knot settled in his belly.

Irish shook his head. "Surely, he's not someone this nut job will be looking for."

"Yeah, most people don't even know where Montana is." Sting Ray snorted. "Much less how to get there."

It was true. Most people didn't want to go to Montana, especially in the winter months when the temperatures got down well below zero. And most people didn't know about the connection Sting Ray had with his Uncle Fred.

His uncle had been the man to raise him when Sting Ray's parents had died in a freak lightning strike while they had been out on one of their weekly date-nights.

"Montana?" Big Bird scratched his chin. "As in Hank "Montana" Patterson's Montana? Is he anywhere close to where your Uncle Fred lives?"

"As a matter of fact, Hank is only about twenty miles from my uncle's cabin in the Crazy Mountains."

"Crazy Mountains?" Big Bird's brows rose.

Sting Ray chuckled. "Yes, the Crazy Mountains are in Western Montana." He shook his head. "I don't think anyone would go after my Uncle Fred."

"And you don't have a girlfriend hidden somewhere we don't know about?" Irish pressed.

Sting Ray gave them a wry grin. "You know the only ones getting any around here, are you two. If I didn't think you guys were serious about this being a real threat, I'd swear you were looking for a way to rub it in about *you* having women and me... not so much."

"Believe me, this is one of those times I wish I didn't have a woman in my life. I hate to think of her being in trouble because of me." Irish pulled into his apartment complex.

Sting Ray unbuckled his seat belt and reached for the door handle. "Couldn't it all be a hoax?"

"Are you willing to blow it off and pretend it's a really bad joke someone's playing on us?" Big Bird asked. He shook his head. "I can't imagine anything happening to Yasmin."

"Or Claire," Irish added.

Or Uncle Fred.

How long had it been since he'd touched base with his uncle?

The man lived in a remote cabin in the mountains. He'd only recently acquired a telephone, after years of living without one. The only reason he had a telephone was because Sting Ray had paid to have the lines and poles installed.

Uncle Fred had insisted he had no use for a telephone, but the stubborn old coot had grudgingly agreed to let it stay, once he'd realized he could talk to Sting Ray whenever he liked. The phone wouldn't chop wood and it wouldn't feed his livestock, which were Fred's criteria for usefulness. But he did like to talk to Sting Ray at least once a month. Granted, the conversations were short. Uncle Fred was a man of very few words.

Sting Ray pulled his cell phone from his pocket.

"You calling your uncle?" Big Bird asked.

"Yeah."

Big Bird and Irish nodded, watching Sting Ray as he held the phone to his ear.

Ring. Ring.

Sting Ray's grip tightened.

Ring. Ring.

"No answer?" Big Bird asked.

Sting Ray's lips thinned. He didn't want to get worried yet. His uncle could be out tending to his cattle. Although at 6:30 in the morning on the east coast, it would only be 4:30 AM in Montana. He could be up that early. If he was, he'd be making coffee and would have heard the phone ring.

"Give it five minutes in case he's in the shower or something." Irish pulled into the parking lot of his apartment. "We'll be right back with Claire and Yasmin."

Irish and Big Bird climbed down from the truck and entered the apartment building.

Sting Ray counted the seconds, trying to wait the five minutes. At three, he dialed his uncle's number again.

The phone rang. It rang again. Then someone picked up. The sound of something crashing against the wooden floor filled Sting Ray's ear.

"Uncle Fred!" he called out. He waited and then tried again, only louder, "Uncle Fred!"

Someone grunted and coughed. Then the sound of the phone's hard plastic casing bumping across the floor preceded the hoarse croak of someone obviously very sick.

"God damn," Uncle Fred said, his voice barely recognizable. Then came more crackling of plastic against hardwood.

"Uncle Fred, this is Sting Ray. What's wrong with your voice?"

"Sicker than a mangy dog." He coughed into the phone.

Sting Ray's gut knotted and a cold chill

slithered across the back of his neck. "How long have you been sick?"

"Just today."

"I'm going to call 911."

"Don't. I'll get over it." He coughed again, sounding like he would hack up a lung in the process.

"Are you in bed?"

"I was."

"Where are you now?"

"On the goddamn," he coughed, "floor."

"Can you stand?"

"No. Just want to sleep. Call later." His voice faded with every word.

"I'm calling the ambulance," Sting Ray said.

His uncle didn't respond. The phone clattered against wood, probably hitting the floor again.

"Uncle Fred!" All Sting Ray could hear was raspy breathing, almost as if his uncle was gurgling.

He hated to hang up, but he did and dialed 911.

When the dispatcher answered, he didn't give her time to say *How may I help you.* Sting Ray said, "This is Ray Thompson. My uncle, Fred Thompson, lives in Eagle Rock, Montana. I was on the phone with him just now, when I think he passed out."

"I can contact dispatch at Eagle Rock and have them check on your uncle," she offered.

Sting Ray gave her the address to his uncle's

place. "One more thing—and this is important— I'm a Navy SEAL just back from a mission involving a dangerous virus. I think someone might have infected my uncle with that virus. When the EMTs go in, tell them it's imperative that they go in prepared with biohazard protective gear."

She assured him that she would pass on all the information. Then she ended the call.

Sting Ray flung open the door, stepped down from the truck and paced back and forth, trying to think of what else he could do. His mind spun around the possibilities.

About that time, Big Bird, Irish and their women arrived at the truck.

Big Bird was first to ask, "What happened?"

"I got ahold of my uncle." Sting Ray stopped pacing and looked Big Bird in the eyes. "He's sick. Really sick."

"What's he doing for it?" Irish asked.

"Not a damn thing." Sting Ray clenched both fists. "I called 911. They'll transfer the information to the dispatch in Eagle Rock and have an ambulance sent out."

"Did you tell them your uncle could be sick with a deadly virus?" Irish's woman, Claire Boyette, asked. "Do they know to go in with protective gear?"

Sting Ray nodded. "I did." He shook his head. "It's not enough. I need to be there."

Irish touched his arm. "We'll get you home. In the meantime, Montana is there."

Sting Ray stared at Irish, trying to understand his friend and teammate when all he could think about was his uncle, possibly dying alone in his secluded cabin in the fucking backwoods of Montana.

"Focus, Ray." Irish gripped his arms. "Hank Patterson is out there. You said so yourself that he was in the same neck of the woods." He glanced over his shoulder at Big Bird.

Big Bird nodded. "Calling." He pulled his cell phone from his pocket and punched the screen.

Hank Patterson was their teammate who'd left active duty to help his failing father and his new fiancé manage their ranches in Montana.

"I'll put a call in to my boss and get them working on who might be responsible for this threat," Yasmin Evans said. As an agent for the CIA, she would have contacts all over the world. Surely they could help find the bastard responsible for the notes and, potentially, for infecting his uncle with a highly deadly virus.

Until now, Sting Ray had believed his uncle was invincible. Despite his lack of affection, the man had always been there for him. When Sting Ray's parents had died in a car crash when he'd only been twelve, his uncle had stepped up to the plate and raised him as his own. Loving or not, the man was Sting Ray's only family. He couldn't lose him.

Sting Ray pushed past Irish and stood beside Big Bird.

"Montana, Big Bird here. Sorry to wake you.

We've got an emergency and need your help." He paused.

Leaning close to Big Bird's phone, Sting Ray strained to hear the conversation.

"Need you to check on Sting Ray's uncle, Fred Thompson."

"Now?" Hank's voice carried enough Sting Ray could hear.

"Yeah," Big Bird said. "Sting Ray called him a minute ago. He was really sick and must have passed out before the call ended."

"Did you call an ambulance?" Hank asked.

"It should be on the way," Big Bird said. "But that's not all."

No longer able to stand on the sidelines, Sting Ray took the phone from Big Bird. "Hank, this is Sting Ray. We think my uncle might be the target of someone who has threatened retribution on us by harming the people we care about."

Big Bird took the phone back. "Sting Ray's the only one of us who hasn't got a girlfriend. His uncle is his only living relative."

"I'll check on him," Hank promised. "He still lives in that cabin in the Crazy Mountains where we went hunting last fall?"

With his head against Big Bird's hand, Sting Ray heard Hank's question and nodded. "Yeah," he spoke loudly enough for Hank to hear. "But be careful. If he *is* infected with that virus, you don't want to bring it back to your wife and new baby."

"Thankfully, they're in California right now. But you're right. I'll take precautions. If I don't go, I'll be sure to send someone who can. We'll handle it and let you know."

Irish took the phone from Big Bird. "Hey, Hank. Irish here. We're coming that way, no matter what. If someone did this to Sting Ray's uncle, he might still be there. We'll let you know our flight details as soon as we know them."

"One of my guys has a sister who works for the CDC," Hank said. "I think she's here on vacation. I'll see what I can do to engage her and the CDC on this. If the virus spreads, there's no telling how many more people will be impacted." Hank's voice was lower and harder. It was his community at stake.

"Be careful out there," Irish said. "I'd stay away from town, and drink bottled water for the time being, just in case."

"That'll be really hard to do. We have the annual rodeo in town and I'm helping out with a chuck wagon."

Sting Ray leaned close to the phone. "For the sake of your wife and daughter, be extremely careful."

"Yeah," Irish said. "I saw what it did to an entire village. Not a soul survived."

"I read you, loud and clear," Hank said. "Believe me, I don't want anything to happen to Sadie or Bella."

Irish ended the call and handed the cell phone to Big Bird. "We've done all we can from here. Let's talk with the boss man and get clearance to go to Montana."

"What about us?" Claire said.

"You're coming, too." Irish slipped his arm around her. "I don't want you out of my sight for a moment." He leaned down and pressed a kiss to her forehead.

Big Bird glanced at Yasmin.

"I'm going, too," Yasmin said. "Maybe if we're in a small town, we'll have a better chance of luring the bad guy and smoking him out."

Big Bird pulled Yasmin into his arms. "Think your boss will let you go?"

She nodded. "If he doesn't, I'll go AWOL." She smiled up at him. "I wouldn't miss this for the world. And I need to keep an eye on you. You might be just as much of a target as Sting Ray's uncle."

Big Bird kissed her on the lips.

Sting Ray's heart pinched. He had to admit, seeing his friends with their women made him wonder if he should give love another try.

Then he remembered how hard it hurt the first time he'd loved and lost.

He shook his head. Love wasn't for him. Especially not now. He had enough on his plate with a terrorist on the loose sporting a virus that, if it spread, could kill the entire population of the United States.

Chapter Two

"Lilly, wake up," a voice said beside her.

Lilly Parker blinked her eyes open and stared up into her brother Tate "Bear" Parker's face. "What time is it?"

"It's 4:35."

She groaned, rolled over in the bed and pulled a pillow over her head. "I'm on vacation. Can't I sleep until at least 6:00?"

"Sorry," Bear said. "There's an emergency situation, requiring your expertise."

"I'm not going snipe hunting in the middle of the night," she grumbled. "Go back to bed."

Bear pulled the pillow off her head. "Seriously, Lilly, this is a life or death situation. I just got off the phone with my boss, Hank Patterson. He said some of the members of his old SEAL team have received threats to their loved ones. One of which is in this area."

Lilly rolled onto her back and rubbed her eyes before giving her brother her full attention. "What does that have to do with me?"

"From what Hank said, the SEALs were involved in destroying a biological weapons manufacturing plant in Africa. Whoever was involved in funding it, or sales of the products, is pissed off. He sent notes to the three SEALS warning them that their loved ones were in danger."

Pushing to a sitting position, Lilly forced the fog of sleep from her mind. "Again, what does this have to do with me?"

Bear shoved a hand through his hair. "I'm not sure, yet. Maybe nothing, but one of the SEALs has an uncle up in the Crazy Mountains not far from here. He tried to call him a few minutes ago to make sure he was all right."

When Bear paused, Lilly hurried him along with, "And?"

"He sounded really sick, and they think he passed out, ending the call. The ambulance is on its way, but they warned them to wear protective gear in case the virus is the cause of his uncle's illness."

Lilly shoved the covers back and swung her legs over the side of the bed. "I didn't bring a protective suit with me. Hell, I'm on vacation."

"Yeah, I know. And I hate to ask, but could you get up to the uncle's house and make an assessment of the situation, even if it's not in an official capacity?"

"No. If you think this could be some kind of terrorist attack, I need to treat it as such and notify the Center for Disease Control immediately. They need to make the call."

Bear handed her a cell phone. "Then you need to contact them. We need you to check out what's going on, ASAP."

She laid her feet on the cool hardwood floor of the house her brother's fiancé had inherited

18

from her parents and was in the process of restoring. Taking the phone from him, she shook her head. "I'm not even sure if my boss is awake at this time."

"Call his home phone." Bear turned and headed for the door. "I'm going to get dressed. I'll meet you at the front door when you're ready."

Realizing her brother wasn't going to take no for an answer, Lilly quickly located her boss's home phone number and placed the call.

He answered on the second ring with a groggy voice. "Lilly? I thought you were on vacation? Why are you calling me at…6:40 in the morning?"

She explained the situation in a few concise sentences. "I need to know if you want me to get involved and, if so, in what capacity?"

"Since you're there now," he said, his voice now brisk, "I want you in the thick of it. I'll clear it with the higher ups. But please, take all precautions. You're one of our best field agents."

"Will do, Phil. I'll report in when I get more information." She ended the call, tossed her cell phone on the bed and hurried toward her suitcase. First day on vacation and she was already back at work. Not that she minded. Since this was her brother's new home, she felt she owed it to him to make sure he and his new community didn't die from exposure to some biological weapon.

Bypassing the new cowboy boots her brother had purchased for her first rodeo, and the jeans she'd planned to wear that day for the parade, she threw on her oldest clothes. If there was a chance of a deadly virus making its way into the community via a sick resident, she might have to destroy her clothing and submit to a decontamination shower to avoid spreading something to others. She'd been in the field often enough, locating the source of plagues, mad cow disease and E. coli outbreaks. Lilly knew the drill and strictly followed protocol. Because she was so vigilant, she had yet to succumb to anything more dangerous than a common cold.

Grabbing her sample kit and a jacket, she hustled out of the room and headed for the door.

Her brother reached it before her and pulled it open.

"You should stay here," she said. "No use everyone catching whatever bug this uncle has contracted." She touched her brother's arm. "No, really. I'd feel a whole lot better if you stayed here with Mia. And don't go out in public."

Bear stepped in front of her. "You're wasting time. I'm going with you. And Mia has agreed to stay here. Not that she's happy about it, but if she has even a slight chance of being pregnant she's not going to be stupid. I don't want her anywhere near this SEAL's uncle, or anyone else for that matter."

Lilly's eyes widened along with her grin. "Are you trying to tell me I'm going to be an aunt?"

A flush filled Bear's face. "No. I'm not saying that. But Mia and I have agreed if such a thing happens and she gets pregnant, we're moving up the wedding date."

"Now, that's good news." Lilly shook her head. "I never understood planning a wedding a year or more in advance. Not that I begrudge yours and Mia's wedding. In fact, I don't remember you ever being happier." She hugged him, ducked around the big guy and hurried out the door. "Just let me handle this."

"Okay, but I'm still going with you."

"Suit yourself." She stepped out onto the landing of the little apartment attached to her brother's house and was met with the cool, pre-dawn of morning. "I have my sample kit, but I'll need a protective suit."

"There will be EMTs at the site. Hank asked that they take an additional suit out there for you."

Lilly chewed on her bottom lip. "I hope their suits are sufficient to protect against biological contaminants."

Bear grabbed her arm, bringing her to a halt. "If you think it's too dangerous, don't go."

"I've been in some pretty hairy situations. Remember, I was on the team tracing the origin of Ebola in Sierra Leone in 2014."

"I know." Bear stared down at her, his brows furrowing. "I can't tell you how many sleepless nights I had." He pulled her into his arms. "You're my only sister. I'd like to keep you around long enough for our children to play together."

She grunted. "You'll be waiting a long time for that to happen. First, I don't even have a husband or a boyfriend. Second, I'm not sure I want to have children. In my line of work, it's hard to deploy to ground zero sites if you have to worry about who's taking care of junior back home." She held up her hand. "Don't get me wrong. I love my job, and I don't want to give it up anytime soon."

Bear nodded. "You're right. Having children isn't for everyone. In fact, I didn't think I wanted children. As a member of Delta Force, you never know if you'll come home in one piece, in multiple pieces or in a body bag."

Lilly patted his cheek. "But you're not a part of Delta Force anymore."

Bear caught her hand, his jaw tight, his grip hard. "Something you need to understand... Once a Delta Force, always Delta Force."

"Hey, brother, you don't have to tell me. You set that little gem of knowledge in concrete in my head a long time ago." She laughed and pulled her wrist out of his grip. "Rest assured, I know. I just wanted to get a rise out of you." Lilly grinned. "And I did. Score one for Lilly." She stared up at her brother. "Are you driving, or am I?"

"I'll drive," Bear said.

"I'd take a vehicle you don't care about, in case they quarantine us and our ride."

"I have an old truck waiting outside."

"Good." She clapped her hands together. "Ready to go?"

Bear nodded. "You bet."

They descended the stairs, climbed into a beat up old pickup and drove out of town.

"You know where this place is?" Lilly asked.

"I do, but I have GPS as backup. Fred's nephew is on his way in from Virginia. From what they said, the virus spreads through the body quickly. If a patient has no quick access to medical treatment, he will die. They aren't even sure medical help will keep a patient alive for any length of time."

"Well, we better hope this man lives. We need to know where he's been and who he might have come into contact with."

"Exactly. The sooner the better. Eagle Rock is already filling up with participants and spectators for the annual rodeo. Folks will be coming in from all over this state and from other states across the nation and Canada. If Fred made a trip to town in the past few days, he could have picked up the virus or spread it to others."

Lilly nodded. "I'll get to work on finding the culprit."

Bear drove them out of Eagle Rock toward the Crazy Mountains. Light was just beginning to edge up over the eastern horizon, bathing the mountains in gray haze. The chill morning air made the windshield fog.

Sitting forward in her seat, Lilly stared out at the mountains ahead. Soon they turned off on a narrower road, and again onto a gravel road.

"Good Lord, how far out does this guy live?"

she asked.

"Way out. From what Hank said, he's a bit of a hermit."

"That's in everyone's favor. If this is an attack with a biological weapon, targeting an introvert is the best scenario for the local population. Then the question is, how the attacker injected the virus into the man's environment."

"Right." Bear's hands tightened on the steering wheel.

"If the attacker wasn't concerned about anyone else in the area, he could have put the virus in the water. Everyone needs water to survive." Lilly stared out at the landscape in front of them. "It really depends on the nature of the virus. Will it survive in water, or is it spread by bodily fluids and contact with others?"

Bear snorted. "You're talking to a layman. I haven't a clue."

"Sorry. I'm just going through different scenarios." Lilly thought back to her studies in Africa on the Ebola virus. "Once the Ebola virus took hold of patient zero, it spread by touch, by coughing, by exchanging bodily fluids of some kind. Bats were the original contributor. They dropped their feces, people walked through the feces and it got passed from one person to another, until tens of thousands were impacted."

Bear shot a glance her way. "I hope that isn't the case here."

Her fingers curled in her lap. "Me, too. If it is, this entire area could be affected. Everyone in it would be subject to quarantine."

Bear checked his GPS and slowed to pull onto an even narrower dirt track. Before he'd gone far, an ambulance appeared in front of them, bumping along the track.

Shifting into reverse, Bear backed all the way out to the road.

Lilly hopped out and waited for the ambulance to come to a stop. She pulled her badge from her pocket and held it up to the driver. "I'm Lilly Parker from the Center for Disease Control. Are you carrying the patient?"

The driver nodded. "He's in the back."

"Condition?"

"Unconscious, still with us, but not looking so good. They've got him on an I.V. for fluids. We'll take him to Bozeman's hospital."

Lilly noted the driver wasn't wearing protective gear.

"Did you come into contact with the patient at all?" she asked.

The driver shook his head. "I stayed in the cab of the ambulance. The guys in the back are in their gear. They know the drill. We're treating this man's affliction as highly contagious."

Lilly nodded, satisfied they were taking precautions. "Do you carry an extra suit?"

He nodded and motioned toward the side panel of the truck. "Dispatch said you'd be coming. There's another suit in the door on my side. Help yourself."

"Thank you." Lilly opened one of the doors,

found the suit and pulled out what she needed in the way of pants, jacket, booties, hood and gloves. Moving as quickly as possible, she finished, shut the door and waved to the driver. They needed to get the patient to the hospital ASAP to improve his chances of survival.

The ambulance rolled away, leaving Lilly to dress quickly in the protective gear. Once she was completely covered from head to toe, she glanced toward the dirt road.

"It's another tenth of a mile up to the house." Bear stood beside her, holding her sample kit, staring up the road that disappeared into the trees. "I'd go with you, but it might be best if I don't."

"Absolutely not," Lilly said. "You're not dressed for the occasion and we don't know what we're working with."

Bear touched her arm. "Be careful. From what Hank said, this is some bad shit."

Lilly nodded. "I will." She took off at a steady pace. The road curved through the trees, completely blocking the view of the house until she rounded a corner and came into a clearing.

A rough-hewn log cabin stood in the middle of the clearing on a slight rise.

Lilly stood at the edge of the tree line, taking in the scene, trying to think like a man set on poisoning a recluse. If Fred hadn't suspected he'd been tainted with a biological weapon, he could have picked it up from anywhere.

Swiping the virus on a door handle or

dropping it into his well water seemed to be the most likely methods of transmission, assuming he hadn't contracted the virus in town. She needed to talk to the patient.

In her line of work, they didn't always get the opportunity to talk with the patient, especially in cases of fast-acting viruses that took down full-grown men within twenty-four hours. If Fred survived, he might be able to shed light on his recent activities.

She drew in a deep breath and stepped into the clearing.

Chapter Three

Sting Ray climbed down from the plane onto the tarmac in Bozeman, Montana. Though he'd had the time, and the seat had been comfortable, he hadn't been able to fall asleep on the trip from Virginia to Montana.

Irish clapped a hand on his back. "Just got a text from Hank. He's already at the hospital. Your uncle is in critical condition in a quarantined area of the ICU. He's hanging in there, but he's in bad shape."

"Thanks for the update." Sting Ray pushed his hand through his hair, exhausted but wired tightly. "Will we be able to see him?"

"Maybe, if you suit up," Irish said. He moved back and held out his hand for Claire as she stepped down from the plane, followed by Big Bird and Yasmin. "If you're ready, our chariot awaits." He tipped his head toward the SUV waiting near a hanger.

As he approached, a tall, blond man with broad shoulders unfolded himself from the driver's seat.

Sting Ray shook his head. "Damn Swede, in all the crap happening in the past few weeks, I'd forgotten you were working with Hank out here." He hugged Axel Svenson, a former member of SEAL Team 10. Having been medically retired from active duty for injuries sustained in an explosion, Swede had come to Montana to work for Hank's brain-child, Brotherhood Protectors. "You're looking good, dude."

"You look like shit," Swede replied and pulled Sting Ray into a hard hug. "Sorry about your uncle."

"Yeah. Me, too." Sting Ray stood back. "I always figured the stubborn old bastard would outlast everyone, if he didn't drop a tree on his own head. I haven't given up on him yet."

Swede's grave face said it all. "Have you heard from Hank?"

Sting Ray nodded. "Yeah. Uncle Fred's in a quarantined ICU and in bad shape." His chest tightened. Though his uncle had never shown much affection, he'd known the old man loved him, in his own brusque way. "Anything on what's wrong with him? Do we know for sure it's the same virus used on the villages in Africa?"

"Not yet," Swede said. "Based on your call, they're treating it as a highly infectious disease and taking all precautions."

"Good."

"They've sent blood samples out on Hank's private plane to the CDC in Atlanta. They have the vials of the virus to compare the sample to. Thankfully, your team was able to collect those vials to give them a starting point."

Sting Ray tossed his duffel bag into the back and climbed into the front passenger seat of the SUV. The other four members of his party loaded their luggage into the rear of the vehicle and got in.

Swede shifted into drive and pulled away from the airport. "We're meeting Hank at the hospital. From there, he wants everyone to stay at his place, until this all blows over."

Irish leaned between the two front seats. "No way. He's got a baby daughter to think about. If we're targets, we can't put Sadie and Bella in danger. If we contract the virus, we don't want to infect his home."

Swede nodded. "Sadie's in California anyway, working on a new movie. Bella accompanied her with her nanny. Hank said he'd have his home fumigated, sterilized and detoxed before they come back."

Irish sat back. "Hank should have gone with them."

Sting Ray agreed. "With a new family, he shouldn't risk catching the virus."

"Claire and I saw what it did to entire villages," Irish said.

Swede glanced into the rearview mirror. "Hopefully, they've been working on a cure or vaccination or something to prevent this virus from spreading. Can't they invent a shot to combat it?"

Sting Ray glanced over his shoulder at Claire, hopefully.

Claire gave them a weak smile. "I haven't been involved in the study. But I'll do what I can. I worked in a research lab for several years before

I signed on with Doctors Without Borders." She shrugged. "Sometimes, it takes years to come up with a vaccine or antibiotics to counteract or prevent the effects of a disease or virus."

His fists clenching in his lap, Sting Ray reminded her, "We may not have years."

"I know." Claire shook her head. "The best we can do for now is to contain it before it spreads."

Sting Ray faced the road ahead. He hadn't been in the affected Somali villages to witness the devastation Irish and Claire had, but from what they had described, not a single soul survived the deadly virus.

Then again, those people hadn't had medical help available, nor had they been able to isolate those infected or identify the method of transmission. If his uncle had contracted the virus, hopefully, the EMT crew's precautions would help to confine it to Uncle Fred. The thought of that deadly virus making its way through the community of Eagle Rock was more frightening than any battle Sting Ray had ever fought. This was an enemy he couldn't see, one that had the potential to decimate an entire town.

When they arrived at the hospital in Bozeman, Hank met them at the front entrance and engulfed Sting Ray in a tight hug. "Hey."

His eyes stinging from emotion and lack of sleep, Sting Ray stood back and shook Hank's hand. "Thanks for stepping in."

"You know I'm here for you," Hank said.

Sting Ray nodded and looked past his friend.

"He's in ICU," Hank said. "You won't actually be able to get inside to talk to him, but you can see him through the window."

Having expected as much, it still bothered Sting Ray that he wouldn't be able to talk to his uncle and reassure himself the old man would in fact pull through. He wanted to believe his uncle was entirely too mule-headed to die. "What do they know so far?"

"Fortunately, we had a biologist from the CDC in the area. She's the sister of one of my agents. She was able to collect samples from your uncle's house. The state helped her set up a special lab for her to work in. She's been studying her samples and your uncle's blood, trying to isolate the virus. She's been at it since early this morning, in constant communication with the CDC."

"Any word yet? Does my uncle have the virus, or is it something else?"

"I don't know. Let's go inside and see if she's come to any conclusions." Hank held the door for the group to enter, and then led them down a hallway, turned to the right and came to a halt at a door. When he lifted his hand to knock, the door opened and a woman dressed in hospital green scrubs stepped out. She had shoulder-length, straight, pale-blond hair and bright green eyes, with dark circles beneath those pretty eyes.

"Ah, Lilly," Hank smiled. "Your timing couldn't be better."

She blinked up at Hank. "Hi, Hank." She stared at the group of people gathered around and sighed. "Can we go where I can find a cup of coffee?"

Sting Ray didn't want coffee. He wanted answers. "Can't the coffee wait? A man could be dying in this hospital. Shouldn't you be more concerned about the potential of a plague, the likes of which we've never encountered, making its way across this country?"

Her brows descended. She looked around at the group and beyond at other people in the hallway. "Look, buddy, if you want to stare at a microscope for hours looking for what, you don't know, hoping to find that unknown something to avoid a catastrophe, have at it." She waved him toward the door. "Otherwise, I'm going for a cup of coffee. Stay or come, I don't care." She marched away.

Hank's lips twitched. "If you want answers, I suggest you follow her, or get ahead of her, and get her that cup of coffee."

Sting Ray's winced. The woman had put him in his place with fiery eyes and a temper to match his own.

Irish grinned and backhanded him in the gut. "Come on, dumbass, you have some apologizing to do." He and Claire followed Lilly.

"I'm not apologizing for the truth," Sting Ray said, his jaw set in a stubborn line, even as he admired the sway of the spitfire's hips as she walked away.

"The truth as you see it," Big Bird said. "I don't know about you, but I want to know what she's found so far. So, suck it up, buttercup." He grabbed Yasmin's hand and followed, leaving Hank and Sting Ray.

"I know you're worried about your uncle. Truth is, we need Lilly Parker's help. Until the CDC can deploy more personnel, she's all we have. She's smart, knows her stuff and has been working since before dawn on this effort without having stopped for food or a drink."

Sting Ray's anger dissipated, and he scrubbed a hand through his hair. "You're right. I was a dumbass. Come on. I want to know what she's found."

Yeah, he had some sucking up to do, but damn it, it was his uncle on life-support and in quarantine with a slim chance of coming out alive.

Chapter Four

Lilly strode to a nearby waiting room. If the rest of Bear's team followed, fine. If they didn't, at least she would be able to get some coffee and infuse a little caffeine into her system to revive her tired brain. She'd been looking through a series of samples under a microscope for the past couple hours and hadn't isolated anything so far. For all she knew, Fred Thompson had a bad cold that had turned into the respiratory infection from hell. However, her gut told her it wasn't just a cold. If his illness was a manufactured biological weapon, the entire town of Eagle Rock would have to be quarantined. Maybe even the state of Montana. The sooner she pinned down the nature of the infection, the sooner they could call in the big guns to help fight the spread. But if it wasn't what she thought it was, she didn't want to stir up drama and send an entire region into hysteria.

The coffee maker in the waiting room looked like it had seen better days and probably could use a good wash. Pulling out a packet of anti-bacterial wipes from her pocket, she removed one and wrapped it around the handle of the carafe. She dumped the coffee into the small sink beside the coffee maker.

"Why did you do that? That was a full pot of coffee?"

The man who'd questioned her commitment to the case, and whose uncle was lying near to death in a quarantine room, appeared beside her. "I don't know who has handled this pot, and I don't particularly want anyone else's germs. Hospitals typically have a nasty collection of germs and diseases. If I can avoid them, I will. Next time, speak up sooner, and I'll save you a cup of poison."

"Thanks. I'm feeling the love." He reached into the cabinet above the coffee maker and retrieved a fresh, pre-packaged coffee filter and grounds and tossed it into the coffee maker.

Lilly paused in her efforts to wash the pot to stare at the man.

He glanced her way. "What?"

She bit down on her tongue to keep from asking the man if he'd washed his hands before handling the packet. Not everyone was as obsessive compulsive as she was. She had to remind herself not to let it bother her. The coffee maker would heat the water hot enough to kill any germs he might have transferred from his hands to the packet. Instead, she bent to the sink and scrubbed the grunge off the coffee pot, then rinsed it in the hottest water she could get from the faucet.

"Hey, by the time you get done with that pot, there won't be anything left of it."

"I like things clean." Lilly filled the pot with water and poured it into the coffee maker. Rude Man still stood close. Too close for Lilly's comfort. She tried not to touch him, but as she lifted the pot, her elbow bumped his chest. Her arm jerked and she spilled water on the counter.

Rude Man covered her hand with his and steadied her aim, guiding the water into the machine. His chest pressed against her back and the faint scent of soap and aftershave filled Lilly's senses and made her hand shake. His fingers tightened around hers and remained there until the rest of the water had made it into the well. Having him stand so close, her hand engulfed in his, was scrambling her normally well-ordered brain cells.

When he removed his hand from hers, she pressed it to her side, curling her fingers into her scrubs, the warmth of his skin still tingling her nerves. Lilly brushed it off as her aversion to swapping germs. Deep down, she knew it was a lie.

Cutting a quick glance his way, she noted the man was tall, with dark hair and intensely blue eyes. A strong chin and square jaw indicated the man could be stubborn. Thick, dipping eyebrows winged up in question or angled downward in a fierce frown in the blink of an eye. He made her uncomfortable in her own skin. Lilly didn't like being uncomfortable in her own skin. It made her feel out of control. And, to her, control was what made her universe manageable. She stepped away from him, and washed her hands again, trying to scrub away the tingling sensation.

"Don't you think they're clean enough?"

Rude man asked.

"Can't blame her," another man joined them. "I've heard about people coming into hospitals with a hangnail and dying from a staph infection." He washed his hands in the sink, dried them and then held one out. "Hi, I'm Irish."

She took his hand. "Lilly Parker."

Irish tipped his head toward Rude Man. "This dumbass is "Ray "Sting Ray" Thompson, Fred Thompson's nephew. He has something to say to you."

Sting Ray frowned at Irish. "I was getting to it."

"By the frown on Miss Parker's face, you haven't groveled enough." Irish punched Sting Ray's arm. "Get to it."

"Jerk," Sting Ray muttered, rubbing his shoulder.

"Dumbass," Irish shot back.

Lilly glanced up at Sting Ray, expectantly.

His lips remained tightly clamped for another second, then his face softened and he gave her a crooked smile. "I'm sorry I questioned your dedication. And thank you for doing what you can to help my uncle."

"There," Irish clapped a hand on Sting Ray's back. "Was that so hard?"

Sting Ray glared at him. "With you making a big deal of it, yes." His gaze returned to Lilly. "But, seriously, there's no excuse for my behavior."

"Damn right," she said. His crooked smile

had left her knees a little wobbly, but his sincerity touched her. "Apology accepted. To keep from staring at the man, she turned to the others of the group who had settled into the waiting room chairs.

Ignoring Sting Ray, Lilly took a deep breath. "I haven't isolated the cause of Mr. Thompson's affliction yet. As you suspected, it appears to be a virus, but I need more time behind the microscope. What I need is my team here. The CDC is gathering one, but it could be another day or two before they can send them out. I don't want to wait to start my investigation, tracing Mr. Thompson's steps to determine ground zero where he contracted whatever it is he has. I can't do that and continue the lab work."

One of the women in the group raised her hand. "I'm Claire Boyette. I'm a medical doctor, but I've worked in a lab, researching diseases and viruses. I could help."

Lilly nodded. "The lab staff here is very helpful, but only used to doing more of the routine lab work they normally encounter in Montana. If this is a mutated virus, created as a biological weapon, they might not know it when they see it." She nodded toward Claire. "I'll work with you to get you started studying the samples, but I really need to get out in the town of Eagle Rock to canvas the locals."

"Miss Parker, they call me Big Bird." He dipped his head. "I'm one of the SEALs involved in destroying the biological weapons manufacturing facility. You should also know that Claire and Yasmin, as our loved ones, are both under the same threat."

"I'll stay with Claire to make sure no one takes a shot at her," Irish offered. "Having Claire confined to a lab will make it difficult for anyone to infiltrate without notice. I can protect her from here."

"Good." Hank turned toward Big Bird. "That leaves Miss Evans."

A dark-haired beauty popped up from her chair, her feet braced for battle. "Please, call me Yasmin. Don't worry about me. I can take care of myself."

Big Bird rose beside her and slipped an arm around her waist. "I know that, but we don't know who's doing this. It could be more than one person involved."

"Spreading a virus can be as simple as rubbing up against someone in a crowd, or coughing within three-feet of another person," Lilly said. "Door handles and handrails are great places to pick up bugs. We don't know if this virus is passed from person to person, or if it's spread through drinking water. If it gets into the drinking water, we need to determine what the shelf-life of the virus is. Does it remain viable forever, or does it have a limited lifespan? Until we know what it is and what its characteristics are, we're shooting in the dark as to how it will be spread."

"She's right," Claire said. "And if you're

targeted, you could contract it and not even know you have it until you've spread it to a number of others. Then it travels fast and the number of people impacted grows exponentially."

"Yeah, and what's making matters worse is that the rodeo is in Eagle Rock this weekend. People began arriving yesterday," Hank said. "They'll be there all weekend and then go back to their homes, their states and countries, depending on where they came from."

Sting Ray's eyes narrowed. "Having the rodeo in town complicates the hell out of finding the one responsible for targeting my uncle. There will be hundreds of strangers in town. How will we narrow it down to just one?"

"We retrace your uncle's steps for the past couple of days," Lily said

"That should be easy. He doesn't go anywhere."

Lilly raised her brows. "Ever?"

Sting Ray's brows knit. "Well, he does like to have coffee in the morning with some of his cronies at the diner."

"Is that all?"

Sting Ray tilted his head, staring off into the distance as if trying to remember. "He occasionally buys feed for his horses at the feed store, if he's out and about anyway."

"That would be a start. I've already gathered samples around the house. We have the blood samples we need from your uncle, but it wouldn't hurt to start there and work our way back to town."

"We can help with the investigation," Hank said. "Two of my guys are away on a mission, but Bear and I can lend a hand canvassing witnesses."

"Just be careful," Lilly warned. "If the virus is spreading, you might become a victim through contact with others."

"Have any other patients presented with my uncle's symptoms?" Sting Ray asked.

Lilly shook her head. "Not so far. But then, he might still have spread it. There could have been an incubation period before it presented outward symptoms. He could have contracted this virus hours or weeks before. We might be tracing it back as long ago as two weeks."

Sting Ray ran a hand through his hair. "Two weeks?"

She nodded. Dear God, even with his hair standing on end, the man was too ruggedly handsome. Her belly tightened. "I need time to brief Claire on the lab work being conducted. I can be ready to return to Eagle Rock in twenty minutes."

"I'll have a chopper on standby." Hank pulled a phone from his pocket and thumbed the buttons on the screen. He stepped away from the others to conduct his conversation.

"Good." Lilly pressed her lips together. "The sooner we get back to Eagle Rock to conduct an investigation, the sooner we can determine a source and a course of action."

"We're with you," Bear said.

"We'll beat this," Big Bird added, lifting Yasmin's hand.

"Damn right, we will," the dark-haired beauty said with a smile, leaning into Big Bird.

Lilly frowned. "Yasmin, you're a potential target. Aren't you afraid you'll be infected next?" She shook her head, rethinking the woman's participation in the investigation. "It's too dangerous."

Yasmin lifted her chin, her dark eyes flashing and her jaw firm. "I'm more afraid of how this could progress. Besides, I'm not good at sitting around twiddling my thumbs."

Big Bird grinned. "True. My woman is kickass." His smile faded, and he turned Yasmin to face him. "But I am worried about you. Sting Ray's uncle is really sick. What if you contract this virus?"

"Then I'll do like I always do and kick its ass." She cupped his cheek and stared up into his eyes. "I'm not leaving you for any other woman to love on. You're pretty much stuck with me."

"I don't want another woman." Big Bird leaned down and brushed a quick kiss over her lips.

Lilly's chest tightened. Witnessing the love in Big Bird's eyes for his woman reminded her of the lack of love in her life. But not all men were like Big Bird and Irish. She knew that first hand. The big SEALs cared about their women, but they didn't make their decisions for them. Some men wanted to completely control you, whether you wanted them to or not. Like her ex-husband. A chill ran down her spine. She fought to keep her body from shaking.

Three years had passed since she'd escaped the horror of her marriage. She never wanted a man to control her again. She had control of her life, now, and she would never let another man take the reins from her.

Squaring her shoulders, she nodded. "Okay. We'll have five of us searching, while we're waiting for the CDC to send more help. What we need to do is retrace Mr. Thompson's steps over the past couple of days. We'll need to document everywhere he'd been and the people he came into contact with. Note everyone. Also, watch for others who might be presenting symptoms like those of Mr. Thompson's: fever, runny nose, sore throat, upper respiratory distress, chills, muscle ache, diarrhea, vomiting and an altered mental status."

"Sounds like the flu," Sting Ray said.

"Many of the symptoms are similar to the flu. The difference is, this could be quick onset."

Hank sneezed and then sniffed.

Every one of the people in the room turned toward him.

He raised his hands. "I'm not sick. I am, however, allergic to hospitals. If we're done here, I have a helicopter waiting to take us back to Eagle Rock."

Lilly's eyes narrowed. "Are you sure you're not sick?"

Claire pulled a pen light from her pocket and advanced on Hank. "Let me check you out."

"Really, I promise." Hank backed away. "I feel fine. No chills, no vomiting, nothing."

Claire continued her advance.

Lilly fought her grin. Based on surface appearances, Hank was indeed fine. But it didn't hurt to have the doctor check him out.

"I'd like to stop in to see my uncle before we go." Sting Ray's breath on Lilly's neck made her hot and cold at the same time. And it made parts of her ache she didn't know could. The man was cranky and stubborn, but the pure alpha male charisma attracted her. Her ex-husband had been an alpha male.

She stiffened. He'd been so alpha, he hadn't let her have a thought or decision of her own. He'd forced her to run everything by him before a decision could be made. At first she'd thought it was cute, and that he cared about her enough to want to make the decisions that were best for her. Before long, he'd made it clear, if it wasn't his idea, it wasn't the right idea. He'd even dictated the outfits she wore.

No thanks. Lilly moved away from Sting Ray, her back straight. If she curled her fingers any more tightly into her palm, she'd draw blood. "Follow me. I'll take you to the quarantined area." She didn't wait for him to acknowledge her statement, but she knew he was behind her, based on the sound of his boots clomping on the shiny tile hospital floors.

45

"I'm coming, too," someone called out.

Lilly glanced back. The entire group filled the hallway. She hid a smile. These people looked out for each other.

When they reached the elevator banks, she stood behind four nurses also waiting for the elevator. A pretty blond in scrubs turned and smiled at Sting Ray. "Nice tattoos. Are you in the military?"

Heat rose in Lilly's cheeks. She wanted to tell the nurses to mind their own business, but they were. Sting Ray didn't belong to Lilly. He was free to flirt with the women. It shouldn't bother Lilly, at all. She wasn't in the market for a relationship.

Been there, done that, had the scars to prove it.

Then why did she want to scratch the pretty nurse's eyes out?

Sting Ray nodded. "Navy."

She smiled wider. "Ooh. I love a man in uniform."

Lilly almost opened her mouth to remind the woman that Sting Ray wasn't in uniform, but bit down hard on her tongue to keep from saying it.

"You're a long way from a port, aren't you?" the blond asked, batting her eyelashes.

Rolling her eyes, Lilly tapped her toe, impatient for the elevator to arrive and end the inane conversation.

Sting Ray nodded, without replying.

Finally, the elevator arrived and the four nurses stepped in.

"We'll wait for the next car," Lilly said.

"No need," said the blond, scooting over to make room. She waved her hand toward Sting Ray. "We have room."

Sting Ray entered the elevator and turned toward Lilly.

She hesitated for a moment, ready to tell him to go on without her, but she couldn't stand the thought of the blonde wrapping her claws around the Navy SEAL's arm. Lilly stepped into the elevator and purposely planted herself between the flirting nurse and Sting Ray.

"We'll catch the next one," Irish said, his lips curling upward. He winked at Sting Ray and stepped back.

The doors closed. Lilly turned her back to the four nurses as the elevator car rose to the next floor.

"Excuse me," the blonde said, pushing between Lilly and Sting Ray. "This is our floor." She slid her hand into Sting Ray's and smiled up at him. "Call me if you need someone to show you around town." She glared at Lilly and left with her three friends giggling behind her.

The door closed.

Lilly fought hard to keep from asking him if he'd call the nurse. It wasn't her business who Sting Ray called. She didn't care. He was a man. She was done with men, other than her brother, who was the only man she needed in her life.

The bell dinged and the door slid open. Lilly stepped out and hurried toward the quarantine room where Sting Ray's uncle had been isolated.

47

She glanced back in time to see Sting Ray toss a business card into the trash.

He caught her gaze and winked.

She turned away before he could see her blush, which, based on the heat filling her face, her cheeks had to be about fire-engine red.

He'd tossed the nurse's number. Why that made Lilly feel better, she didn't know.

Not interested, she reminded herself. *Not interested.* If she reminded herself often enough, she'd get over the attraction she was feeling toward the man following her.

She stopped at the glassed-in area where Mr. Thompson had been isolated from the rest of the patients in the hospital. "This room is the quarantine room. It has its own ventilation system that will not feed into the rest of the hospital."

Sting Ray stepped up to the window and stared into the room where his uncle lay on the bed, hooked up to an IV, ventilator and a full array of electronics to monitor his pulse, blood pressure, oxygen and anything else they could think of to monitor.

"Is he going to make it?" Sting Ray asked, his voice low, his gaze pinned to the man on the bed.

Lilly nodded to the nurse fully covered in protective gear. "They're taking good care of him."

"Will all that stuff they're wearing keep the nurses from catching whatever he has?" Sting Ray asked.

His concern for the healthcare workers

warmed Lilly's heart. "It should. They've improved protective gear since the Ebola outbreak. They learned a lot from that event."

Sting Ray nodded. "Has he woken up since they brought him in?"

Lilly shook her head. "They're doing everything they can to help your uncle."

The Navy SEAL inhaled deeply and let go of the breath before he turned to face her. "I'm going to kill the bastard who did this to my uncle."

"We're still not entirely sure he's infected with the virus from the factory in Ethiopia. He could just be sick."

Sting Ray sighed. "I'm betting it's more than that."

"You must care a great deal for your uncle."

"He's all the family I have in the world. I'm not losing him to someone's plan for revenge."

Lilly's estimation of the initially rude SEAL raised a notch as she glanced back at the man lying motionless on the hospital bed. Sting Ray loved his uncle. Her heart squeezed hard in her chest. Sometimes good medical care wasn't enough. "You might not have a choice."

"Well, the sooner we find him, the sooner we can put a stop to the spread of the virus. Irish said it didn't discriminate over who it killed. He'd run across an entire village of dead people." His brows descended, and he reached out to clamp his hands on her arms. "I want to catch the son-of-a-bitch who dared to bring it to my hometown and the people of Montana. I need you to help me do that."

Lilly stared up into incredibly intense, blue eyes. Her stomach clenched, her pulse fluttered and she had to swallow hard to push words past her tightened vocal cords. "We'll find him," she found herself promising. "But you have to let me go."

He glanced down at his hands on her arms and let go immediately. "I'm sorry."

She rubbed the skin where his hands had been and backed away, her pulse still racing. "I'll do the best I can to find the source."

The rest of the group arrived in the hallway, crowding around the glassed-in room. They all talked at once.

A nurse stepped up behind them. "I'm sorry, but you'll have to leave. This is a hospital, not a concert hall." She ushered all of them back toward the elevator, with a stern, no-nonsense expression on her face.

Sting Ray stopped at the nurses' desk and jotted down his phone number. "I'm Mr. Thompson's nephew and his only living relative. "Call me with any news on his condition, please."

The nurse nodded. "We will."

Sting Ray glanced at his friends gathering in the elevator. It was full. "I'll take the stairs."

Lilly waved at them. "I will, too." The door closed, leaving Lilly and Sting Ray alone.

The navy guy glanced around for the stairs. "This way." He strode toward a door marked

EXIT and opened it for Lilly.

She led the way downward, highly aware of the man behind her. When they reached the bottom, the rest of the team waited.

"Let me spend a few minutes with Dr. Boyette, showing her where everything is."

Hank nodded. "We'll be waiting out front."

Irish escorted Lilly and Dr. Boyette to the lab where they'd given Lilly an isolated room to work with the blood samples they'd taken from Mr. Thompson. Irish left them to suit-up in protective gear, standing outside the room, his arms crossed over his chest, daring anyone to get past him.

"How well do you know Sting Ray?" Lilly pulled on a fluid resistant suit and matching booties.

"I've known him for a couple weeks. Since they all got back from a mission to Africa. I met Irish in Somalia." Dr. Boyette smiled, shaking her head. "He saved my ass from an al-Shabaab terrorist. While we were on the run from al-Shabaab, we came across a couple of villages of dead people. Our journey led us to a factory in the middle of the Ethiopian desert. Sting Ray and the rest of the team helped to destroy the factory manufacturing the biological weapons. After that, Sting Ray, Big Bird and Irish went after a shipment of the vials and successfully recovered them." Claire stepped into protective pants and pulled a top over her head. With her protective hood in her hands, she faced Lilly. "They're the real deal when it comes to heroes."

51

Lilly blinked. "Wow. I didn't know. All I knew was their loved ones were targeted by a psycho. And you're one of them. Loved ones. Not psychos." She smiled at the pretty doctor, and then pulled on her hood.

"Yeah, I kinda like Irish. And he likes me." She pulled on her hood. "He'll protect me no matter what. He's done it on multiple occasions, risking his life in the process. He'll take care of me. Besides, I don't think anyone could get into this area unnoticed."

"I hope so. I hate to think of whole towns decimated by this disease." Lilly pulled gloves over her hands.

"Me, too." Claire pulled on her gloves. "Ready?"

"Ready." Lilly led the way into the inner room where her microscope was set up along with the vials of Mr. Thompson's blood and samples from Thompson's home. She showed Claire what she'd done so far. Once she was certain Claire knew what she was doing, Lilly left her to it.

Lilly stripped out of her protective gear and placed it in the appropriate disposal area along with her scrubs. She then stepped into a shower, scrubbed her body, hands and everything else, dried and dressed in a fresh set of scrubs.

When she exited the room, she ran into Irish.

He stepped aside and glanced over her shoulder at the inner door, a worried frown denting his forehead. "Is she all right?"

Lilly nodded. "She's wearing protective clothing. When she comes out, she'll go through the correct protocol to ensure her safety and that of others."

Sting Ray stood close by. "Are you ready?"

"Yeah." She followed him out of the hospital to a waiting SUV and slid into the middle seat, scooting as far over as she could to allow Sting Ray to sit beside her.

His thigh touched hers and set off all kinds of electrical impulses she was totally unprepared for. If sitting beside Sting Ray was going to make her that uncomfortably aware of him, she wasn't certain she should be teamed up with the SEAL to conduct the investigation.

Chapter Five

The helicopter was on loan from the local Army National Guard aviation unit. Hank had pulled strings to get it, telling them it was an opportunity to get some flying time in. The Blackhawk's interior was large enough to transport Sting Ray, Lilly, Hank, Big Bird, Yasmin and Lilly's brother, Bear.

Sting Ray sat beside Lilly, determined to stick to her like Velcro. The woman knew the questions to ask and how to conduct an investigation to locate the source of what had put his uncle in the hospital.

The headsets they all wore did little to drown out the roar of the rotors. The trip to Eagle Rock was conducted in silence. Sting Ray went through the thousand and one scenarios that could have taken place in order to infect his uncle with a killer virus. That no one else, so far, had presented with the symptoms was a blessing he hoped would continue. But it would make it harder to trace the source back to the originator.

The helicopter landed in an open field on Hank's and his wife Sadie's ranch. As soon as they disembarked the chopper took off.

Hank waved them toward the big ranch house. "Come on in. I'll get keys to vehicles you can use." He glanced at Lilly. "I think I can find clothes for you to wear. Sadie won't mind loaning them to you. Anything to make sure her home is safe when she gets back from LA with Bella." He winked.

The group trudged into the house and waited while Hank took Lilly into his wife's closet and told her to pick something that fit. Sadie wouldn't be angry.

Once Lilly was dressed, she emerged from the master bedroom and joined the others, feeling a little more confident dressed in snug-fitting jeans and a sweatshirt.

Hank collected keys for two vehicles. "Lilly, you and Bear can have this one. It's four-wheel-drive in case you need to get up to Sting Ray's uncle's house. I understand it's on a pretty rugged road."

Sting Ray intercepted the keys. "I'll drive for Miss Parker. I'm familiar with the area."

Bear nodded. "You got it."

Lilly's lips pressed together, but she didn't say anything.

"Actually, I'll keep Bear with me," Hank said. "I have most of my guys in the field on missions of their own. I could use Bear on the phones and computers, searching the data for a clue as to who might be behind these threats."

Bear nodded. "I have some friends at Langley I can contact."

"Good," Hank said.

Yasmin stepped forward. "I'll have my boss check with his sources to see if intelligence has linked anyone from the Saudi Prince's palace with the sale of the virus vials."

Hank lifted a phone from its cradle. "You'll have to use land lines. Cell phone coverage this far from town is iffy at best."

"In the meantime, Miss Parker and I will get started on the investigation." Sting Ray hooked Lilly's arm and started for the door.

As soon as they were out of sight of the others, Lilly dug her feet into the smooth wooden floors. "Look, Mr. Thompson, I'll go when I'm good and ready."

"It's Sting Ray." Sting Ray frowned. "I thought you were anxious to get started."

"I am. But get this straight." She poked a finger into his chest and lowered her voice to just above a whisper. "I don't like being ordered around or manhandled."

Sting Ray stared into her eyes and saw something more than anger. Her whisper had been a little shaky and her bottom lip trembled ever so slightly.

Holy shit. Was she afraid of being bossed around? He stared down at the finger pushed against his chest. He encircled it with his own, and squeezed gently and let go. "I'm sorry. I shouldn't be so pushy. You're the expert. I'll do whatever you say." He dropped his hands to his sides. "And I promise not to touch you…" He curved his lips into a smile. "Unless you want me to."

"Trust me, I won't want you to." She looked

away too quickly, her cheeks blooming with color.

She was blushing. Sting Ray's blood warmed. Was she attracted to him, but afraid to admit it? Hell, he was attracted to her and her no-nonsense approach to solving the problem they faced.

"We should get going," Lilly said. "It's already after noon, and I want to talk to people before they all go home or to their hotels, or wherever they go in this godforsaken place."

He chuckled. "Hey. You're talking about my home."

She shot a glance back at him. "No offense."

"None taken. The Crazy Mountains aren't for everyone."

She stepped out of the ranch house, heading toward the driveway, all the while staring at the mountains rising up around them. "They are beautiful."

"The Crazies have a way of growing on you," he said softly.

Her lips quirked. "People or mountains?"

Sting Ray grinned. "Both."

"Did you grow up here?" she asked.

"Partly."

Lilly frowned. "Explain."

"I moved to Eagle Rock—my uncle's cabin in the woods—when I was twelve."

Her frown deepened. "Did your parents move in with your uncle?"

"No. They died in a car wreck on the way home from a night out with friends in Seattle. I was at a friend's house, camping in their backyard when I found out."

Lilly stopped so suddenly, Sting Ray ran into her. He grabbed her shoulders to keep her from being knocked to the ground. Once she was steady, he released her. "Sorry. I've already broken my promise not to touch you."

She shrugged, rubbing her arms where his hands had been. "It's okay. I shouldn't have stopped so fast." Lilly resumed walking. "I'm sorry about your parents. It must have been a big shock to you."

"It was. We were a happy family. My mom and dad felt lucky to have me. Though they tried for more children, they couldn't get pregnant, so they showered me with all their attention. I was well-loved and content with our life in Seattle."

"Then you moved to the backwoods of Montana," Lilly concluded.

"With an uncle I didn't know." He shook his head. "I had only met Uncle Fred once when we'd come out to Montana to visit the National parks. He was my father's older brother. He had a beard, wore old clothes and smelled of sweat. I couldn't comprehend how he was my father's brother. They were so different. My father was an accountant. My uncle...well, he lived off the grid, raising his own food or hunting for it."

Lilly climbed into the passenger seat of a four-wheel-drive, black SUV.

Sting Ray slid behind the steering wheel, started the engine and shifted into reverse. When he did, he put his arm over the top of her seat and twisted toward her.

"It might help the investigation if I knew more about your uncle." Lilly's cheeks turned a pretty shade of pink, and she stared out the front windshield as if trying not to look his way. "Was your uncle married? Did he have children of his own?"

With a wry grin, Sting Ray glanced her way. "No."

She tilted her head, her brows wrinkling. "Then, why did he take you in?"

Shifting into drive, Sting Ray pulled away from the house and drove down the road to where it connected to the highway. "My uncle might have been a hermit, and didn't much care for most people's company, but he had a strong sense of duty. He took me in when he didn't have a clue how to raise a child, because he was my only family. He didn't believe in dumping a kid into the foster system if there was family capable of taking care of him."

"Noble of him."

Sting Ray snorted. "I wonder if he really knew what he was getting into. Hell, I was half-grown and already pretty set in my ways."

"Seems to me, a man who lived off-grid wouldn't know what to do with you." She stared across at him, her lips twisting.

"He didn't know what to do with me. He gave me a room in his house, put food on the table that he'd killed, cleaned and cooked himself and thought that was all he had to do."

A soft chuckle reached Sting Ray's ears. Lilly smiled. "I take it you had quite the adjustment?"

"To say the least. I'd never met a more crotchety old man. He never smiled, never hugged, never gave me a word of encouragement."

"Which your parents had done so many times before, I take it."

Sting Ray nodded. "I missed them so badly that first year, I wanted to join them."

Lilly sucked in a sharp breath. "Taking your own life doesn't make things better."

"I know. About the time I thought I couldn't take it anymore, my uncle took me deep into the Crazy Mountains on a camping trip. I thought he was taking me out in the woods to lose me. I wasn't happy, and I wasn't above telling him about it."

She glanced his way, her gaze locked on his face. "What did he do?"

"He took me fishing in a lake I never would have seen had I refused to go. It was high in the hills, and the only way to get to it was by hiking in. It took us two days of climbing to get there."

"And when you did?"

"I had never seen anything so beautiful. I was tired. My feet hurt and the backpack made my shoulders ache, but when we came out of the woods beside the small lake, it was like walking into heaven."

"Sounds amazing," Lilly said.

He sighed. "It was, and then some. I don't

think I realized just how special that day was until I left Eagle Rock and joined the Navy."

"Did your uncle say anything while you were fishing?"

"No. He just got to work catching crickets and digging for worms." Sting Ray remembered that day like yesterday. The air was cool on his cheeks and so clean it almost hurt him to breathe it. The clouds reflected off the still water of the snow-fed lake, and the sun shone down, warming them. "I figured I might as well find my own worms. My uncle wouldn't dig them for me. A few minutes later, we were sitting on a log by the shore, with our lines in the water. We didn't speak, just fished. What we caught, we cooked on a campfire and ate."

"Have you been back to that lake since then?"

Sting Ray shook his head. "No. But I stopped feeling sorry for myself and got on with living. I found that working hard wasn't as bad as I'd thought. I learned how to garden and can the produce by watching my uncle. He rarely said anything. Hugs were few and far between, and he never told me he loved me."

"That had to be hard, coming from loving parents."

"Yeah. But it made me tougher. I don't think I would have made it through BUD/S training if I hadn't learned what I did from Uncle Fred."

"He sounds like a special man."

"He's a hard man to get to know. I'm still not

sure I completely understand him." Sting Ray snorted. "He never talked about himself or his past. And before my parents died, I barely knew he existed. I was too wrapped up in my own life to care to ask about him."

"Sometimes, you wish you could have a do-over to make things the way they should have been," Lilly said, quietly, staring down at her hands in her lap.

Sting Ray would have asked her what she would have done over, but they'd arrived at the edge of Eagle Rock. Traffic thickened, bringing them to a standstill on Main Street.

"Rodeo?" he asked, frowning at the inconvenience.

Lilly nodded. "It wasn't as bad before dawn when we drove through town."

"Where should we start?"

"I've been to your uncle's house in the mountains. You mentioned something about a feed store?"

Sting Ray chuckled. "Anytime we came to town together, Uncle Fred made a point to stop at the feed store first. He knows the owner, and he occasionally played checkers with whomever was sitting on the porch."

"We'll start there. Maybe the owner or workers can remember when and where he was and who he might have come into contact with."

"With the rodeo in town, it could be a huge challenge to narrow it down to any one person. There are hundreds of participants and their support crews milling about town, eating at the cafes and talking to anyone who will give them the time of day."

"We won't know until we start asking," Lilly said.

Sting Ray pulled in front of the feed store, but couldn't find an empty space. He drove around the side of the store, parked and got out.

Lilly didn't wait for him to come around to the front of the vehicle. She hopped down, strode toward the feed store, climbed the stairs and entered.

Sting Ray followed, admiring the sway of Lilly's hips and the determination with which she attacked the task ahead. She would be a force to be reckoned with.

Inside, local cowboys and ranchers wandered the aisles, shopping for things they needed for their ranching operations. Rodeo participants searched for items they'd forgotten or ones they had broken or lost, anxious to make their purchases and get back to the rodeo arena located at the county fairgrounds.

Sting Ray studied every person he passed, wondering who they were and if one of them was the guy who'd infected his uncle. He hurried to catch up to Lilly.

She'd made a beeline toward the checkout counter, and smiled at the old man waiting for the next customer. "Good afternoon."

The old man returned her smile with a straight face and no animation in his expression.

"What can I get you?"

She studied the man for a moment and then turned toward Sting Ray. "My boyfriend and I need to ask a few questions."

Hearing Lilly call him her boyfriend had a rippling effect on Sting Ray's pulse. It made him wonder what it would be like to be Lilly's boyfriend. Not that he was interested in making her statement real. He wasn't sure he had what it took to be anyone's boyfriend. It had been a long time since his parents' deaths. Sure, they'd been a loving couple, but his uncle hadn't been a model of care and concern. As a result, Sting Ray found himself standoffish with women. Yeah, he'd slept with a few, but never felt a desire to be with them for more than a night. Not one of them had sparked anything more than lust in him.

"What kind of questions?" The worker behind the register frowned across at Sting Ray, his eyes narrowing. "Do I know you? You look familiar."

"Hello, Mr. Bergman." Sting Ray stuck out his hand. "I'm Fred Thompson's nephew, Ray. I used to come in here with him when I was in high school."

Mr. Bergman took his hand and gave it a firm shake. "You joined the military, didn't you?"

"I did. The Navy." Sting Ray released the older man's hand.

The old man's frown was back. "I heard Fred got sick and was rushed to the hospital last night."

Sting Ray nodded. "He was."

Bergman shook his head. "You'd have never known he was sick. Why, he was out on the porch yesterday morning playing checkers with Charlie Hughes. He seemed fine then. Was it his heart?"

"No. We don't know what it is, yet."

"Keep us informed," Bergman said. "I'll have the missus put him on the prayer list at church."

"Thank you." Sting Ray tilted his head. "Actually, we think he might have picked up a bug from someone, and we were retracing his steps to make sure no one else is sick. Have you seen Charlie today?"

The feed storeowner shook his head. "Not yet." He glanced down at his watch. "He usually shows up in the morning and plays checkers on the porch with whoever shows up, or plays by himself." Bergman glanced right and left and then leaned toward them. "Charlie's getting older, you know. I think he's starting to show signs of dementia. He and your uncle used to be old poker buddies."

"I didn't know that," Sting Ray said. His uncle had gone out every Friday night, but had never told him where he went. He'd leave him reading a book or working with the horses. Hearing that his uncle had a friend he visited, made Sting Ray realize that his uncle wasn't quite the recluse he'd always thought he was.

"Were there any other people around my uncle or Charlie?"

Bergman shook his head. "I couldn't tell you that. I only saw them briefly. Things have been

65

pretty busy around here, what with the rodeo in town and all. I've been opening early and staying open late to help out. There's been a lot of strangers coming through the store. Any one of them could have stopped and talked with Fred and Charlie."

"Mr. Bergman, where does Charlie live?" Lilly asked. "We'd like to check in on him. Just to make sure he didn't get whatever Uncle Fred has."

"Two blocks from here." Mr. Bergman gave them a street address. "He always walks here. Calls it his morning constitutional."

Lilly smiled. "Does he live with anyone? A wife or one of his children?"

"He's all alone," Mr. Bergman's lips pressed together. "I believe that's why he likes to sit on the porch here and play checkers. I think he's lonely since his wife died six years ago."

Another customer lined up behind Sting Ray with an armload of items.

Sting Ray held out his hand again. "Thank you, Mr. Bergman. Please, tell your wife we said hello, and that my uncle would appreciate any prayers she'd like to send his way."

Sting Ray followed Lilly out of the feed store and down the steps.

She paused with her hand on the door handle of the SUV, waiting for Sting Ray to unlock the door.

"Do you want to walk, or drive the two blocks?" he asked.

Lilly dropped her hand. "Let's walk. We can study more people at ground-level."

Sting Ray fell in step beside her as they walked the two blocks to Charlie's street.

The sidewalks and streets were crowded with cowboys, wearing jeans, boots and cowboy hats. As far as Sting Ray could tell, none of them had so much as a sniffle. They all appeared to be there for the rodeo. A few wore baseball caps, and the women wore everything from jeans to short denim skirts. Most wore cowboy boots and had long hair.

Lilly didn't wear cowboy boots, and she didn't walk with the swagger of the women affiliated with the rodeo. She strode down the block with a firm step, her gaze on the people around her—determined to find the man responsible for infecting Uncle Fred.

This woman was like a dog with a bone. She wouldn't give it up. Not until she had what she'd come for. Answers.

Sting Ray found that sexier than any other quality. The woman had grit. He found himself admiring her more and more. Which couldn't be a good thing. He wasn't in the market for a permanent relationship. He'd spent too much time with his uncle, learning to be distant and unresponsive. A woman like Lilly needed a man who could show her the love she deserved.

Chapter Six

When they reached the crossroads of Main Street and the street Mr. Bergman had indicated, Lilly glanced back at Sting Ray.

He nodded.

She didn't hesitate, but continued to march forward on her investigation.

He'd been right with her from the moment they'd stepped off the helicopter, sticking to her like flypaper. Used to working with a team, Lilly found it comforting to have him along with her. Two pairs of eyes looking at the problem was always better.

At the same time, she was comforted, she was also disconcerted. The man made her blood hum and her lady parts tighten. Yeah, he was handsome as the devil, and his eyes seemed to see right through her. Could he tell that he turned her on? Would he make a move on her because of it, even though he'd promised not to touch her unless she wanted him to? Hell, at that moment, she was beginning to regret telling him not to touch her.

Then again, she had a job to do. Starting something with Sting Ray wasn't in the playbook. She had to remain objective and clear-headed.

The house Bergman had indicated was a rundown, dilapidated home with peeling paint and rotting eaves. The steps up to the porch had several brand-new boards in between those faded gray by weather.

Lilly laid her hand on the rail and climbed the stairs. The rail wobbled beneath her touch, causing her to stumble.

Sting Ray reached out to steady her, the hand on her arm warming her more than it should, sending heat flowing southward, low in her belly. She shot him a tight, wry smile. "Thanks."

Shoot! Had she willed herself to stumble so that he would touch her? That didn't make any sense. Sting Ray was a Navy SEAL. He would only be there long enough to see that his uncle and the people of Eagle Rock were safe. When the dust settled, he'd be on his way back to his unit, and Lilly would be on her way back to Atlanta to work with the CDC. Even if she wanted, there could be no future for her and the handsome SEAL.

Hurrying forward, she raised her hand to knock on the outside screen door with its torn mesh and broken handle. The front door jerked open before she could tap her knuckles on the wooden doorframe.

"What do you want?" the man demanded, his bushy brows dipping low over the bridge of his nose.

Lilly gave the older man a gentle smile. "Are you Charlie Hughes?"

"Yeah. So?"

She turned to Sting Ray and opened her

mouth, but didn't get the chance to say anything.

"Mr. Hughes," Sting Ray jumped in, "It's good to see you. You might not remember me. I'm Fred Thompson's nephew, Ray." Sting Ray gave him a smile that melted Lilly's knees. "We hope you don't mind, but we'd like to ask you a few questions about my uncle."

"Fred, you say? You're Fred's nephew?" The man squinted through what was left of the ripped screen. "You don't look like little Ray Thompson."

Sting Ray chuckled. "I've grown up."

"I'd say you have." Charlie opened the door. "If you're Fred's nephew, you can't be all bad." He narrowed his eyes to slits. "You aren't selling anything, are you?"

"No, Mr. Hughes. We're not selling anything."

The older man's face cleared, and he stepped back. "Come in, come in. I didn't get the chance to go to the feed store today. Not feeling well."

Lilly's pulse quickened, and she shot a quick glance at Sting Ray before turning her attention to the old man. "Mr. Hughes, we're sorry to hear you're not feeling well. Could you tell us what's wrong?"

He shrugged. "I don't have anything physically wrong with me. It's just..." He turned away and lifted a paper from a hallway table and stared down at it. The page was worn and yellowed with age and appeared to be a clipping from a newspaper. In the middle of the clipping was a photograph of a young woman. Based on her hairstyle and clothing, the photo could have been from the fifties. "I just didn't feel like company." He held out the article.

Lilly took it and read about a woman named Eileen Hughes who'd died six years previously. The article was an obituary, the month and day of the woman's death coincided with the current month and day. "Was this your wife?" Lilly asked.

Charlie nodded. "Eileen was such a pretty young thing. You can't tell from the picture, but she had fiery red hair and a great big heart. How she ever fell for me, I'll never know." He drew in a deep breath and let it out. "I thank God every day I had her as long as I did."

Lilly's heart squeezed hard in her chest. "I'm sorry for your loss, Mr. Hughes."

He shrugged. "At least, she died peacefully in her sleep." He glanced around as if looking for something and finding nothing. "I miss her."

"I'm sure you do. She must have been amazing." Lilly handed the obituary back to Mr. Hughes.

"She had to be, to love me. I was no prize catch." Charlie hugged the article to his chest and turned away. "Please, come in. I don't have much, but I can offer you a cup of coffee."

"No, thank you," Lilly said.

Sting Ray raised his hand, shaking his head. "I can't do the caffeine this late in the afternoon."

Charlie led them to the kitchen anyway and sat in a metal chair with red vinyl cushions, at an old-fashioned, Formica-topped table. He waited for them to sit, and then asked, "What brings you here?"

Lilly leaned forward. "Mr. Hughes, did you visit with Fred Thompson yesterday?"

Charlie nodded and smiled. "Old Fred is one of maybe three people who stops long enough to play a game of checkers with me in front of the feed store. Never mind I always beat him, but he doesn't seem to mind." He frowned across the table at Lilly. "Why do you ask?"

"We were just curious. You know he's sick in the hospital, now, down you?" Sting Ray asked.

Charlie shook his head. "Fred? That man's never sick. He came to see me when I was in the hospital for pneumonia. He brought me a magazine and my own pajamas. I can't tell you how grateful I was that I didn't have to wear that hospital gown."

"Did Fred seem ill when you were talking with him?" Lilly asked.

Charlie snorted. "Fred doesn't talk much. He just seems to show up when you need him most." The older man tilted his head. "As for sick, I don't recall him sniffling, coughing or anything else. He looked like the same old friend he's always been. He fixed my front step. A sick man wouldn't do that, would he?"

Sting Ray smiled. "Probably not. When did he fix the step?"

"Yesterday, after I beat him at checkers." Charlie leaned across the table with his hand cupped around his mouth. "I bet him I'd win. He said that, if I won, he'd fix my step." Charlie leaned back, grinning. "I won, and he fixed my step."

"Was there anyone else hanging around you two at the feed store, or who followed you back to your house?" Lilly asked. "A stranger, maybe?"

Tilting his head again, Charlie tapped a finger to his chin as his gaze drifted to one corner of the room. "I can't recall. With the rodeo in town, a lot of strangers have been in and out of the feed store. Bergman's business booms at this time of the year." Charlie's eyes widened. "I'm sorry. Eileen will have my hide if I don't offer you a drink. Would you like some coffee or tea?" He rose from his chair and hurried toward the coffeemaker. "Normally, I would offer a beverage right away. Eileen taught me well. She's such a good host."

Lilly's chest tightened at the old man's words. His mind had drifted. She couldn't imagine how deeply he must have loved his wife to be unable to let go of her. "It's okay, Mr. Hughes. You offered coffee when we came through the door. We declined."

He faced them, a frown pulling his brows downward. "I did?"

Lily nodded. "Yes, you did. Eileen would have been proud."

His expression cheered. "Oh, good. I can't seem to remember what I did in the past five minutes, much less thirty years ago."

"It's okay." Lilly reached out to pat the man's arm. "We all forget."

He lifted the obituary from the table, and his smile faded. "Eileen died today. I don't know what I'll do without her."

Lilly's gaze shifted to Sting Ray.

His face was set in hard lines, his jaw tight. "Mr. Hughes, we have to go. Is there anything you need before we leave?"

"Would you like a cup of coffee?" he asked, his face hopeful.

"Not right now, thank you." Sting Ray stood and held out his hand. "It was good to see you again."

"You look familiar," Charlie said. "Do I know you?"

"Yes, sir, you do." Sting Ray touched the old man's shoulder. "I'm Fred Thompson's nephew."

"But you're so big," Charlie shook his head. "Ray is a little boy."

"I grew up," Sting Ray repeated without showing any irritation.

Lilly's heart swelled at how patient Sting Ray was with the older man's memory loss. "Thank you for letting us visit, Mr. Hughes. We have to be on our way now."

"Please come back and stay a little longer next time." Charlie followed them to the door and held it open while they passed through.

The old man's hopeful smile tugged at Lilly's heart. Once they were out of earshot, Lilly commented, "Mr. Hughes is a nice man. I didn't recognize any of Fred's symptoms in him. I hope he doesn't get whatever your uncle has contracted."

"Me, too." Sting Ray shook his head. "I always thought my uncle was a hermit. I didn't know he came to town every other day to play checkers and fix porch steps."

"We think we know people, but sometimes we don't." Good and bad. She'd had the experience of the bad. Fortunately, Sting Ray was learning good things about his uncle.

"What now?"

She sighed. "You said your uncle also frequented the diner?"

"Yes, he did. But he was also interested in the rodeo. My uncle was a bull rider back when he was younger. He won a collection of buckles he kept in an old Army footlocker. He never talked about his rodeo days. Hell, he didn't talk much about anything. It's possible he might have gone to talk to some of the bull riders coming into town for the rodeo."

"Where are they having the rodeo?"

"At the fairgrounds."

"Walking distance?" she asked.

Sting Ray lifted his eyebrows. "I guess it wouldn't hurt. It's on the far side of town." He paused and rubbed the back of his neck. "If we knew what our terrorist looked like, this could be a whole lot easier."

"No kidding."

They walked in silence. Lilly stared into every

face she passed, wondering if the cowboy with the big black hat could be a terrorist in disguise. Or if the pretty blonde with the tight jeans and low-cut blouse was the one who'd infected Fred. None of the rodeo cowboys seemed dangerous enough to be their man. And none of them were sick like Fred.

Lilly prayed the sickness was confined to Fred, and that he'd pull through, for his nephew's sake.

Chapter Seven

At the fairgrounds, Sting Ray spotted Big Bird and Yasmin talking to a gun dealer. Big Bird held a hunting rifle with an impressive scope in his hands.

Sting Ray grinned. Big Bird had a collection of rifles in a gun safe back at his apartment.

"Isn't that your friend Big Bird?" Lilly asked. "Let's check in with them and see if they've come up with anything."

Sting Ray caught Big Bird's attention and waved him over.

His tall friend laid the rifle on the table and thanked the dealer before ambling over to where Sting Ray stood with Lilly.

"Anything?" Sting Ray asked.

"We were questioning the man selling guns," Big Bird said.

"He says he's been selling guns for the past two years," Yasmin added.

Big Bird handed a business card to Sting Ray. "He's prior military. A marine. Saw action in the Middle East and got out after three deployments."

"Why would he be interesting to us?" Lilly asked.

Big Bird's gaze met Sting Ray's. "He spent time in Djibouti before he got out of the military."

"So?" Sting Ray shrugged. "We were there, too. But we're not terrorists."

"Yeah," Big Bird said. "While he was there, he could have established contacts with the Ethiopian Prince Yohannis, the man whose palace housed the biological weapons manufacturing facility."

"It's a stretch," Yasmin said. "But so far, it's all we've got. How about you?"

Sting Ray shook his head. "All we know is my uncle played checkers on the porch of the feed store yesterday around noon, and then may or may not have gone to fix a friend's porch step."

Big Bird frowned. "What do you mean, may or may not?"

"The friend has dementia. He can't remember if it was yesterday that my uncle fixed his porch or another day. He did say that my uncle was never sick and was fine yesterday when he played checkers."

Lilly added, "Again, we don't know if that was yesterday or another day. The feed store owner did verify Fred was at the store and did play checkers yesterday with the local with dementia."

"Were you able to verify any other contact with anyone else?" Yasmin asked.

Lilly shook her head. "No. Have you run across anyone with the same symptoms?"

"No," Big Bird confirmed. "I feel like we're searching for the needle in a haystack."

Sting Ray's cell phone vibrated in his pocket. He fished it out and looked at the number on the screen. "It's Hank. He wants us to meet him at the diner."

"Might as well," Big Bird said. "I'm not so sure this effort is getting us any closer."

"True," Yasmin agreed. "It's getting late and I'm hungry. Perhaps Hank has something for us to go on."

As they made their way toward the fairgrounds exit, a chanting crowd surged toward them bearing signs that said, STOP ANIMAL ABUSE and FREE THE BULLS.

"What the hell?" Sting Ray muttered, trapped by the mass of protestors.

Lilly shouted over the chanting. "PETA protestors."

Big Bird glared at the horde, wrapped his arm around Yasmin and plowed through.

The thought that the People for the Ethical Treatment of Animals protest would be a good cover for a terrorist attack crossed Sting Ray's mind. He, too, wrapped an arm around Lilly and pushed his way through the throng, breaking free as they reached the gate to the fairgrounds.

"That was nuts." Lilly stepped away from Sting Ray and pushed a hand through her hair.

Yasmin smiled up at Big Bird. "I knew there was a reason to keep you around. You make a great bulldozer in a crowd full of activists."

A van stood nearby with the name of the local news station painted in bold letters across the side. A man stood beside it, his hands on what appeared to be a video game control device. He stared up at the sky.

"Drone," Big Bird said, pointing at the small aircraft hovering over the protestors.

Sting Ray glanced up at the drone and paused beside the man controlling its flight. "Is your drone equipped with a camera?"

He nodded, grinning. "Yup. I'm getting all this on it, as we speak. Who knew you could get paid to have this much fun?"

Lilly grabbed Sting Ray's hand. "Come on, a lot of folks are headed toward the diner. Hank might have some important information for us."

They hurried up Main Street to the diner and entered. The place was crowded with rodeo goers and locals.

Hank waved to them from a large table on the far side of the restaurant. Bear was with him.

Sting Ray followed Lilly, held her chair for her and then seated himself between her and Hank. Big Bird and Yasmin took the chairs across from them. A waitress arrived at their table with menus and coffee mugs. After she'd taken their orders for drinks, she disappeared.

"What have you got?" Sting Ray asked.

Hank's face was grim. "Dr. Boyette has been working with the CDC contacts Lilly gave her and positively identified Fred Thompson's virus as the same one from the vials recovered in the Saudi Prince's palace in Riyadh."

Sting Ray's heart turned a cartwheel in his

chest, and his belly knotted.

Yasmin muttered a curse.

Lilly reached for Sting Ray's hand beneath the table and squeezed it. "We knew there was a good chance of a match, given the threat."

"Yeah," Big Bird said. "But I had hoped Mr. Thompson simply had a nasty cold, and he'd get over it soon enough."

"The question is when do we call in the big guns?" Sting Ray asked.

"One patient doesn't make an epidemic," Lilly reminded them.

"Dr. Boyette said that, so far, Mr. Thompson is the only patient who has presented with symptoms. The hospital is on high alert and will notify the good doctor and us if anyone else comes in with the same symptoms."

"That's good to know. What about the patients who think it's only a cold and stay home to fight it?" Yasmin asked.

Sting Ray nodded. "From what Mr. Bergman said, my uncle was at his store yesterday, showing no signs he was even sick. This virus works fast."

"The good news is that Dr. Boyette tested Mr. Thompson's well water and found no signs of it there. So far, the water supply appears safe."

"But for how long?" Bear asked. "If the terrorist turns the virus loose in the water supply, everyone in Eagle Rock, and more downstream, could be infected."

"We'll keep tabs on the water with frequent testing," Hank reassured them.

81

The door to the diner opened and a man in a county sheriff's uniform entered with one other dark-haired man dressed in dark slacks and a black leather jacket. The men glanced around the room, their gazes stopping at the table where Sting Ray and their group sat.

"I think we have company," Sting Ray said.

Hank turned toward the men making their way across the room. "Good, maybe Sheriff Wilson knows something. We alerted him to what was going on when we called 911 this morning."

Sheriff Wilson stopped next to Hank and held out his hand. "Hank."

Hank stood and took the sheriff's hand. "Sheriff."

"DEA sent a reinforcement." Sheriff Wilson turned toward the man with him. "Marcus Faulkner—Hank Patterson, former Navy SEAL."

Sting Ray, Big Bird, Bear and the women all stood and faced the men.

Hank performed the introductions, and they made room for the two to take a seat at the table.

"We had news from the hospital," Hank said and briefed them on what Dr. Boyette had discovered with the help of the CDC. "My question for you, Miss Parker, is at what point would we quarantine the entire town?"

Lilly shook her head, her lips pressing together. "For now, we don't have an epidemic. We have one patient infected. Isolating that patient is about the best we can do until more people present with the symptoms. We don't know enough about this virus."

"You know it decimated an entire village in Africa," Yasmin said.

"True, but we don't know how it was spread, and we do know the village was poor and didn't have access to the kind of healthcare you can get here in the States. Mr. Thompson is the first man to come down with the virus. Until he gets better or..."

"Dies?" Sting Ray's fists clenched.

Lilly nodded. "Or dies. We won't know how this virus will respond to treatment. Isolation and quarantine can be tricky and could be considered an infringement on civil liberties."

"Miss Parker," Sheriff Wilson leaned closer to her and spoke softly so that his voice wouldn't carry to other tables nearby, "We have a rodeo going on. The potential to spread this virus could be catastrophic when these people head home to their towns or states."

She nodded. "It's risky. But until we know more, we don't really have a choice. One man sick doesn't make an epidemic."

"I'm here to help in any way I can," Faulkner said. "I can interview suspects if you need me to."

"We have to *have* suspects. So far, none have materialized," Bear said.

Yasmin shook her head. "We're shooting in the dark. We don't know who could have been involved with the manufacturing facility or the sale of the vials of virus."

Sting Ray tapped his fingers on the table, his

thoughts going back to the deserts of Africa and Saudi Arabia. "Whoever it is has to be an American with connections to both the Ethiopian facility and the House of Saud."

"I have my contacts working on that." Yasmin shook her head. "I haven't heard anything yet."

Hank stared hard at her. "How are you feeling?"

Yasmin smiled. "I'm fine. So far, I haven't been hit." She tipped her head toward Big Bird. "I have my bodyguard protecting me."

"Not that she needs it," Big Bird said.

Hank nodded. "I'm not sure it's a good idea for you to be walking into the crowds. Anyone could be out there ready to take you down."

"I'm tough, and I have an iron constitution," Yasmin said, her eyes narrowing. "I once did a force march with pneumonia and a sprained ankle. I can kick a puny little virus's ass."

Lilly shook her head. "Let's hope you don't have to. We don't know if Mr. Thompson is going to make it, even with the best medical help."

"My uncle is one tough son-of-a-bitch. My money's on him pulling through." Sting Ray prayed he was right. For all of them. If one virus could knock out an entire village, it was bad. Really bad."

"In the meantime," Faulkner said. "I'll work through my higher headquarters to see what they come up with. Between the DEA and the CIA, we should have some potential suspects they've been watching."

"Great. We can use all the connections we can get." Hank stared around the table. "We're working with a ticking time bomb. The sooner we disable it, the better.

He didn't have to tell Sting Ray. His uncle was proof. "Let's get back to work."

"It's getting dark. Yasmin and I will get back to the rodeo. Events will be going for another hour or two."

Sting Ray stood and held out his hand. Lilly placed her hand in his. "Miss Parker and I will go to the local watering hole. Maybe someone will stand out there."

"Don't you want to eat first?" Bear asked, his gaze on his sister.

"We'll catch something at the tavern," Lilly said. "I feel like we're running out of time."

Hank stood with them. "You'll need rest. You're welcome to bunk at the ranch, but you might prefer to stay in town. We're expecting thunderstorms in the area tonight."

"They can stay in the upstairs apartment at my place," Bear said. "Lilly has a key."

"Where will you be," Lilly asked her brother.

"I'll be at Hank's ranch," Bear said. "We have the computers set up to monitor data. I need to be near them to catch anything coming across."

"The storms will make for a muddy mess at the rodeo," Sting Ray commented.

"And make it harder to tromp around

questioning people," Lilly said. "We'd better do what we can tonight."

"Agreed." Big Bird rose beside them.

Yasmin joined him. "We're on our way, as well."

"If you need me, I'm rooming over the tavern." Faulkner pushed back from the table and left.

Big Bird led the way to the diner door.

The PETA crowd had migrated from the fairgrounds, parading down Main Street and bringing traffic to a complete standstill.

Big Bird barreled his way through, dragging Yasmin behind them.

Lilly followed Yasmin, and Sting Ray brought up the rear, bumping into people, being hit in the face by signs and generally being annoyed at the amount of time it was taking to go two blocks.

Halfway to the tavern, Lilly tripped and fell to her knees. Sting Ray squatted beside her. "Are you okay?"

"I'm fine, just clumsy."

Ahead of them, Yasmin yelped and slapped her hand to the side of her neck. "Damn it!"

Sting Ray jerked Lilly to her feet.

Two yards ahead of them, Yasmin stood still in the middle of the crowd, her hand clamped to her neck.

Big Bird used his body to block others from running into her, growling at anyone who dared.

Sting Ray and Lilly caught up and surrounded the woman.

"What's wrong?" Lilly asked.

"I don't know." Yasmin still held her hand to the side of her neck. "I think I was stung."

"Let's see." Lilly reached out to lower Yasmin's hand, and gasped.

A tiny dart, no bigger than a wasp with a fluffy tail clung to the column of her throat.

Lilly ripped off her jacket and used it to pull the dart from Yasmin's neck.

"Is that what I think that is?" Sting Ray asked.

"If you think it's a blow dart, that's what it is." Lilly stared down at the dart nestled in her jacket.

Sting Ray spun in the direction the dart would have come from, searching the crowd for someone with anything that looked like a blow dart straw. All the people he could see were carrying signs, not even looking at them. Dusk had settled in the valley, turning the sky to gray. A shadowy figure slipped around a corner, out of sight.

"Take care of her," Sting Ray ordered.

"Where are you going?" Lilly called out after him.

He didn't slow down to explain. He had to catch up to that figure before the man got away. Pushing and shoving his way through the sign-bearing masses, he finally reached the alley the man disappeared down. It was empty. He ran to the end of the building and spotted the same figure racing to the end of the next street.

Sting Ray raced after him.

Chapter Eight

Lilly bundled the dart into her jacket. "We have to get Yasmin out of this crowd ASAP and call 911."

"Damn it to hell." Big Bird growled. He scooped Yasmin up in his arms. "This can't be happening. I promised to protect you."

"Yeah, well, shit happens," Yasmin said. "Put me down. I can move myself."

"Not as fast as I can move you." Big Bird pushed his way through to the sidewalk and down a deserted side street.

Lilly pulled out her cell phone and dialed 911, gave the dispatcher directions to get to them via the less crowded back streets and warned them to dress for contagious conditions. When she hung up, she dialed Hank and apprised him of the situation.

Moments later, Hank and Bear arrived. A siren wailed from the far end of Main Street, heading their direction.

"Where's Sting Ray?" Hank asked.

Lilly held the jacket away from her body, careful not to let the tiny dart touch her with the dreaded virus. "He ran after someone."

Bear stood back from Lilly. "Are you all right? Do you think you're exposed?"

"I doubt it. Yasmin is definitely exposed, but

the dart went into her, not us. She probably won't be contagious at first. But if it replicates quickly, it won't be long. You two better go."

"Not without you," Bear said.

"I think I'll be okay," Lilly said, "as long as the ambulance gets here quickly. I'm more worried about Yasmin."

"I'm fine." She scratched the wound on her neck, and frowned.

Lilly studied the area surrounding the pinprick, without getting too close. "It's getting red around the spot where the needle penetrated."

"You all might want to stand away from me," Yasmin said her voice not as strong as it had been. "I don't want you to get sick as well."

"I'm not going anywhere," Big Bird said.

Yasmin turned her frown on him. "You need to help them with this investigation. If you stick around me, you'll catch this nasty bug." She swiped her hand across her nose and sniffed. "Go."

Big Bird shook his head. "No can do. I'm staying with you."

Hank took several steps backward and nodded. "Yasmin's right. Even though she might be infected, she needs a bodyguard to keep anyone from taking a second shot at her. When Fred and Yasmin both pull through this, the terrorist will be pissed off and ready to take it a step further."

"Now, we know it's not any safer to be in a crowd. We need to warn Irish to be extra vigilant with himself and Dr. Boyette. This guy might get frustrated and go after the SEALs next."

"Let him." Big Bird's lips curled back in a feral snarl. "I'll kill the bastard."

The ambulance pulled up on the street behind them. EMTs leaped out, suited up and advanced on them.

A few minutes later, Yasmin, along with the jacket containing the dart, were loaded inside and carried to the hospital. Big Bird accompanied her, leaving Hank, Bear and Lilly.

"Are you sure we're not contagious?" Hank asked.

"Yasmin would have had to sneeze or spew bodily fluids on us," Lilly said. "We're okay, for now. But whoever did this could target any one of us next. We have to find him soon."

Hank glanced around. "Which way did Sting Ray go?"

Lilly pointed. "He ran down an alley headed south. Other than that, I don't know."

"You two head back to Main Street so he can find you," Bear said. "I'll go south and see if he needs help."

Hank touched Lilly's arm. "Come on. I don't want to leave you alone."

"Why?" she said. "I'm not the target. I don't mean anything to Sting Ray, Big Bird or Irish."

"Yeah, but you might be targeted for association. You've been with Sting Ray all day. The man who shot that dart might have been aiming for you."

Lilly thought about that, and her stomach clenched. "I tripped right before it happened. Sting Ray dropped down beside me almost immediately. Yasmin was hit about the same time."

Hank's jaw tightened. "Did you see anyone?"

"No. I couldn't see over the signs and heads of the protestors."

Hank frowned. "In that case, how would the shooter have picked you out?"

Lilly's eyes widened. "Unless he was shooting from above."

"Let's head back to Main Street and look." Hank led the way. When they reached the main road through town, he put out his arm. "Wait here."

The parade of protestors had moved on or dissipated, leaving only a few people walking by.

Hank stood in the middle of the road and looked in all directions. Streetlights had come on, making golden circles of light on the sidewalks. A moment or two passed before Hank waved Lilly forward.

She joined him and glanced up at the buildings to the west, the direction from which the dart had come.

The general store with its faux front loomed over them. Beside it stood a two-story building. The downstairs rooms were an antique shop. The upstairs had curtains hanging in the windows, possibly an apartment. On the other side of the general store stood a two-story colonial home with a wide front porch, the front porch light on, casting a friendly glow.

Hank shot a glance to the south. "I don't see them."

Lilly chewed on her bottom lip. What if the dart shooter had targeted Sting Ray? "Should we go after them?"

"Bear will find him. Let's check out those buildings." Hank crossed the street and circled the general store.

Lilly followed, studying the exterior, searching for stairs, ladders or anything someone could use to climb up to the top. The general store had none of those.

"If someone wanted on top of this building," Hank noted, "they would have had to get there from the inside."

Lilly nodded and turned to the antique shop. At the rear of the building was a set of stairs that led up to an entrance to the apartment. Hank climbed the steps and tried the doorknob. He shook his head and called out, "Locked." Raising his fist, he knocked.

Lilly held her breath, praying the shooter wasn't on the other side of that door.

A few moments passed.

Hank started to turn away when the door opened a fraction and an older woman's head peered out. "Can I help you?" she asked.

Lilly craned her neck, straining to hear the conversation on the landing above.

"Sorry to bother you, ma'am," Hank said.

"But I wondered if anyone had been up here fifteen minutes ago besides you?"

"I've been here all evening. Alone. Why do you ask?"

"We were looking for someone, but I must have the wrong apartment," Hank said. "Again, I'm sorry to disturb you."

The woman closed the door, and Hank descended, shaking his head. "I didn't see any other way to the top of the building."

"Let's check the one on the other side of the store." Lilly hurried around the back of the general store to the stately colonial home. A FOR SALE sign lay on the ground behind the home as if tossed there in a hurry.

Gooseflesh crawled across Lilly's skin as she approached the back door.

Hank hurried up the back steps beside her and arrived there first. The door stood ajar, the doorframe splintered. He raised his finger to his lips and drew a pistol out from beneath his jacket. "Stay here," he whispered.

Lilly's pulse thundered against her eardrums. She'd worked in Africa where she'd been escorted from place to place by armed men. That had been years ago, and not in the United States. This kind of shit didn't happen in the States, did it?

When Hank disappeared into the house, she sucked in a breath and held it, counting the seconds until he returned, all the while wondering how Sting Ray was doing. Could the shooter still be in the house? Could there be more than one?

Was Sting Ray off on a wild-goose chase?

She strained to hear footsteps inside the empty house. Surely some would echo off the wooden floors she could see through the open door.

Without her jacket, the chill night air and her rising tension made her shiver.

Something clattered inside, making Lilly jump. Afraid Hank might have been hurt, she started for the door, but a sound behind her made her turn. A hand snaked out and clamped over her mouth, another circled her, pinning her arms to her sides. She tried to scream, but couldn't get the sound past the palm. Then breath warmed her ear, and a voice whispered. "Shh. It's me."

Her knees buckled and she would have sunk to the wooden deck if Sting Ray's arms hadn't been holding her up. He pulled his hand away from her mouth, turned her to face him and touched her lips with his finger. "Hank in there?" he asked, his voice so low, only she could make out his words.

She nodded.

"I'll go." He started around her.

Lilly shot out a hand, grabbing his arm. "He's got a gun."

Sting Ray nodded and eased into the house as silent as a shadow.

Again, Lilly held her breath. This time hoping the two men wouldn't kill each other. Glad he'd found her, Lilly wasn't happy he'd gone in after Hank. A minute passed. Halfway into the next, the door swung open, and the two men emerged.

Sting Ray came out first, shaking his head. "Our guy was here."

Hank held up a piece of toilet paper with a drinking straw pinched between his fingers.

So relieved they were all right, Lilly flung her arms around Sting Ray and clung to him for a moment, remembering how to breathe.

He chuckled. "Worry about me much?"

"Hell, yeah," Lilly exclaimed. "What if you had run into the shooter? What if he'd tagged you like he did Yasmin?"

"Then I guess I wouldn't be helping you find him. Hank would have to take over." He bent to brush a quick kiss over her lips and straightened.

Shocked at the contact, Lilly touched her fingers to her mouth and stared up at him. "Why did you do that?"

"I was worried about you, too. When I got back to where I'd left you, everyone was gone."

"Did you catch the guy you were chasing?" Hank asked.

Sting Ray shook his head. "No. He got away. I followed him several blocks, but he was always ahead of me. Then he just disappeared. I went up and down several streets but never picked up his trail." He slipped an arm around Lilly's waist and pulled her against him. "I was worried he'd circle back to you."

Lilly leaned into him. She'd told him not to touch her, and here she was wanting to crawl all over the man. What did that say about her? That she was a hypocrite? She was needy? Or she was just plain crazy and possibly falling for this man she'd only met that day. Or maybe it was all those things. Whatever it was, she needed to get a grip and move away.

Later. After her heartbeat returned to normal.

"Let's get back to the main road. Bear should be headed back by now."

"Where did he go?" Sting Ray asked.

Hank grinned. "Looking for you."

They stepped out of the alley between the general store and the white colonial home in time to find Bear coming up the sidewalk from the south end of town.

"Bear and I will head back to the ranch," Hank said. "We need to check in with my contacts and see if they've come up with names of people who might have connections to Prince Yohannis of Ethiopia and anyone inside Prince Khalid bin Abdulazi's palace in Riyadh."

"Lilly and I will be at the tavern, looking for clues," Sting Ray said.

Lilly nodded, still too shaky to participate in the conversation. She'd get her head back on straight soon enough. In the meantime, she liked the reassurance of Sting Ray's solid set of muscles against her side. She'd like it even better if she could feel her skin against his.

Sting Ray didn't remove his arm from around Lilly as they walked the few blocks to the tavern. Once inside, they had to wait a few minutes for a table to empty so that they could be seated.

A man sat on a stool on the stage, playing an acoustic guitar, singing old ballads. Some people faced him, listening while others ignored him completely, caught up in describing rodeo events.

A waitress stopped beside them. "If you don't want to wait, two seats opened up at the bar."

"That would be perfect." Sting Ray tucked his hand beneath Lilly's elbow and escorted her to the empty seats. He leaned close and whispered in her ear, "We'll have a better vantage point from the bar, and bartenders are usually full of information."

She nodded and smiled across the counter at the bartender. "Could I have a light beer on tap?" she ordered.

"Make that two," Sting Ray added.

Lilly's brows rose. "I didn't picture you as a light beer drinker."

Sting Ray patted his flat abs and winked. "Even SEALs have to watch their weight."

She shook her head. "Not buying it."

The bartender arrived with two mugs filled with frothy beer, and set them on the counter.

"Sir," Sting Ray said when the man would have turned away.

The bartender stopped and faced Sting Ray. "I'm not a sir. I work for a living."

Sting Ray chuckled. "Point taken." He nodded toward the tattoos on the man's forearms. "What branch of the military?"

The bartender's eyes narrowed. "Army. Special Forces." He snorted. "A hundred years ago." He nodded toward Sting Ray. "You?"

"Navy."

"Squid?" He thrust his hand over the counter. "Lance Franklin."

Sting Ray gripped it and felt his bones being crushed. He applied enough pressure to let the former Special Forces man know he wasn't a pansy-ass. "Not a squid...frog."

The man's eyes widened, and he gave Sting Ray a wry grin. "SEAL?"

Sting Ray nodded. "Mind if I ask you a couple of questions?"

The man shrugged and rubbed a rag across the counter. "Shoot."

"You know a man named Fred Thompson?"

"I do. He comes in here once or twice a week for Jack Daniels on the rocks." His brows dipped. "Why?"

"He's my uncle."

The brows lifted. "You must be the nephew he talks about. *When* he talks. For the most part, he's pretty quiet. He's proud of you."

Sting Ray felt the bartender's words hit him square in the chest. His uncle had never told him he was proud of him. To hear it from someone else...Well, it was one more side of his uncle he hadn't known existed. Was the old man as grumpy and non-communicative as Sting Ray had originally thought?

"I haven't seen him today, but he was in here

yesterday." Lance pulled glasses out of a dishwasher and dried them before stacking them beneath the counter. "Had his usual."

"Did he seem okay to you?" Sting Ray asked.

Lance shrugged. "Yeah. He was talking about you."

"To you?" Lilly asked.

"No. He was talking to someone next to him. I just happened to overhear him say something about his nephew."

Sting Ray's heart stuttered and raced ahead. "Do you remember who he was talking to?"

Lance glanced around the crowded room. "Don't know his name. Probably one of the cowboys with the rodeo."

Sting Ray turned around. "Is he in the room now?"

Again, Lance looked around the barroom, his hand still on the glass he was drying. Finally, he said, "No. I don't see him."

"Would you recognize him if you did?" Lilly asked.

"Probably." Lance's eyes narrowed, and his gaze moved to a high corner of the room. "He had brown hair, dark eyes and a tattoo of a scorpion on the inside of his wrist."

"Have you seen him in the tavern today?" Sting Ray asked.

"He was here a little while ago."

"How long ago?"

"Maybe an hour. I don't remember. It was crazy busy in here." Lance chuckled. "Still is."

Again, his eyes narrowed, and his brows dipped. "Why? Did he do something to your uncle? Because Fred's a good guy. I don't stand for bullies in my bar."

"Maybe. We're not sure yet," Sting Ray said.

The bartender tilted his head and picked up another glass. "Where is Fred?"

His jaw tightening, Sting Ray's gaze met Lance's. "In the hospital in Bozeman."

Lance slammed the whiskey glass he was drying onto the counter. "Fuckin' hell. What happened?"

Sting Ray was surprised the glass didn't shatter. He leaned forward and dropped his voice so the others around them wouldn't hear. "He's contracted a potentially deadly virus. We think someone tagged him with it."

Lance straightened. "You think the guy with the scorpion tattoo might be infected as well?"

"No, we think whoever infected my uncle is targeting individuals."

"No fuckin' way." Lance dipped his hands beneath the faucet and rinsed them thoroughly. "Why haven't they called in the Army National Guard and put Eagle Rock in quarantine?"

"Because we're containing the individuals who have been affected," Lilly said. "So far, no one else has presented with symptoms."

"You mean we have to wait until more people are infected and possibly die of this shit before they shut down the town?" Lance shook his head. "That makes no sense."

She nodded. "That's why it's imperative we catch the guy who's doing this before he becomes indiscriminate with the people he infects."

"Well, goddamn, I'll nail the bastard to the wall if I see him again."

"We don't know he did it. But it would help if you'd let us know if you see him in here again. We could pull him in for questioning." Sting Ray reached for a napkin and quickly wrote down his cell phone number.

"You bet. I'll keep my eyes peeled and my nun-chucks polished."

Sting Ray smiled. He appreciated the man's enthusiasm for catching the terrorist. He only hoped the bartender didn't get hurt in the process.

So, for the first time that day, they had a clue. The man who could have infected Uncle Fred sported a scorpion tattoo on the inside of his wrist.

Sting Ray lifted his beer mug at the same time as Lilly did. Together, they swiveled on their seats and faced the barroom.

They'd find the Scorpion and take the bastard down.

Chapter Nine

After two hours of staring at every person entering and leaving the tavern, plus the early morning wake-up call, Lilly hit the stamina wall and knew if she didn't get some sleep, she would be of no use to anyone.

She scooted off the bar stool, stood and stretched. "I have to call it a night."

The crowd in the barroom had thinned to only a dozen people, cradling their drinks and talking to friends. "I think it's highly unlikely Scorpion will come to the bar this late. If he does, Lance has your number, he can call. We can be here in just a few minutes."

"I take it we're staying at your brother's house?"

Lilly nodded. "We need to be close to town in case something comes up that needs our immediate attention." She glanced up into Sting Ray's incredibly blue eyes and almost melted. As tired as she was, it wouldn't take much to fall into bed with this man.

"You need some sleep. The sooner the better." He held out his hand. "Ready to go?"

"Way past ready." She yawned, covering her mouth with the inside of her elbow, then laid her hand in his. "If I have to look at one more brown-haired man's wrist, I'll faint."

"My brother's house is three blocks from here." Lilly weaved her way through the tables and chairs toward the exit. "Should we collect the SUV from where we left it at the feed store, first?"

"I think it makes sense, in case we need to make a quick getaway."

Lilly moaned. "I thought you'd say that. I was hoping it would magically appear in front of my brother's house." She sighed. "Well, let's do it before I fall asleep on the sidewalk."

He held out his hand.

Lilly placed hers in his, liking how warm and strong it felt wrapped around her fingers.

Yeah, she could get used to having the big SEAL around on a more permanent basis. Too bad neither one of them lived there or even close to each other. Even if she wanted something to happen between them, their lives wouldn't come together. She worked out of Atlanta. He was out of... She snorted softly. Hell, she wasn't sure where he was stationed. It hadn't come up in any conversation.

Using the excuse of relying on his protection, she leaned into the man, soaking up the heat of his body, getting as close to him as possible as they walked the several blocks to the feed store. The SUV stood where they'd left it on the far side of the feed store what felt like days ago but was only a few hours. No other cars or trucks were parked around it.

Sting Ray opened her door for her and

helped her up into the seat. Then he closed the door, rounded the hood to the driver's side and climbed in. "You know, I spilled my guts about my pathetic childhood, what about you?" He paused with his hand halfway to the ignition.

She stiffened for a moment, then closed her eyes and leaned her head back against the headrest. "What's to tell?"

"I've spilled my guts about me. It's only fair you reciprocate." He stared across at her. "Hell, I don't even know if you're married."

She laughed. "Rest assured. I'm not. Anymore."

Sting Ray inserted the key in the ignition. "I take it you were married at one time." He paused and glanced toward her. "Divorced or widowed?"

He wasn't going to give up, was he? Lilly sighed. "Divorced."

"I'm sorry."

She opened her eyes and stared straight into Sting Ray's eyes. "Don't be. My divorce was the best thing that ever happened to me." At the time, it hadn't felt that way. It had been hard standing her ground against her ex. He'd yelled, cursed and belittled her until she'd felt like nothing.

"Your choice or his," Sting Ray asked.

She smiled. "Oh, it was mine. All mine. And he wasn't happy about it at all. He couldn't control me ever again."

Sting Ray's eyes narrowed. "Is that why you don't like to be touched? Did he hurt you?" The

SEAL's jaw tightened and a muscle twitched in the side of his cheek. "If he did, I'd be happy to break every bone in his body."

Warmth filled her heart. She believed him, and it felt good to know someone had her back. "Thanks. But that chapter of my life is over. I never have to see him again."

"The offer is still open if you need it. Anytime. Any place." Sting Ray jammed the key into the ignition and twisted. "No woman should ever have to fear a man's touch."

The engine didn't turn over.

Lilly heard nothing but the click of the starter.

Sting Ray tried again and got the same response. It was as if it didn't have a good connection on the battery or the battery was dead.

"Stay in the car," he said. "I'll check it out."

He searched for the hood release lever, pulled it and waited for the corresponding pop. The hood opened a fraction of an inch. Sting Ray climbed down from the SUV.

Lilly opened the door on the other side and climbed down, joining him at the front of the vehicle. "Do you know how to fix engines?" she asked, fiddling with the controls on her cell phone.

Sting Ray ran his hand along the bottom of the front grill, searching for the latch to open the hood.

Lilly knew every carmaker seemed to put the latch in a different place. "Here, let me shine a light on it." Lilly activated her smart phone's flashlight and squatted in front of the hood. "I think it's up here."

Sting Ray dropped to his haunches and looked where she shined the light.

As Lilly reached for the latch, she noticed something that looked like a damp cloth draped over the handle. Before her hand could touch the cloth, Sting Ray grabbed her wrist, yanking it back. "Wait."

Her heart flipped several times and she pressed her hand to her chest. "Why? What's wrong?"

He took her cell phone from her and shined the light at the rag. "Who puts a rag on the latch to open the hood of a vehicle?"

Lilly shrugged. "Someone who doesn't want to get dirty?"

"It's loose. It would have fallen off while driving." He shined the light over it again. "And it appears to be damp."

Lilly rose to her feet and stepped back. "You think it's contaminated with the virus?"

"I'm not willing to find out." Sting Ray stood and looked around. "But we can't leave it there. What if someone else finds it?"

"I have a mask, a pair of latex gloves and plastic bags I carry in case I need to collect samples." She pushed him behind her. "Let me handle this."

"Lilly, the guys who collected Yasmin were dressed from head to toe in protective suits. Do you think a mask and gloves are enough?"

She sighed. He was right. Even tired, she should know better than to touch anything as dangerous as the virus. "You're right. Call the EMTs. We'll have them transport the sample to Dr. Boyette at the Bozeman Hospital."

Forty-five minutes later, after the cloth had been removed and bagged and the SUV had been wiped clean with disinfectant, Sting Ray drove to Bear's house and parked under a brightly lit streetlight.

By then, Lilly was so tired, she could barely keep her eyes open.

The apartment she'd been staying in was on the second floor, accessible from the outside, up a set of stairs that seemed to go on forever.

"I don't have pajamas to offer you," she said.

"I sleep nude." Sting Ray scooped her up in his arms and carried her up the stairs without breaking a sweat. Of course, the temperatures in the Crazy Mountains had been near freezing every night since Lilly had arrived.

She was cold, tired and a little glad of Sting Ray's he-man, take-charge attitude. It got her up the stairs faster. But being crushed against his chest also made her ultra-aware of the man, his muscles and how much she wanted to touch them without the barrier of his shirt and jacket between them.

Had she lost her mind? Or was she just so tired, she was delirious?

Blaming her delirium on exhaustion, she

wrapped her arm around Sting Ray's neck and let him be the strong one and carry her all the way to the door. She took the key from him, inserted it into the lock and pushed the door open.

"You know you don't have to carry me," she said, snuggling close to him as he crossed the threshold into the quaint sitting room with its medium-sized sofa. An interior door led into the single bedroom with the king-sized bed covered in an old-fashioned quilt and half a dozen fluffy, white pillows.

All thoughts of sleep flew from her mind, and her blood flowed like hot mercury through her veins. And it was headed south to her core.

As Sting Ray set her on her feet, Lilly rested her hands against his chest, staring at them, not up into his face. Could he see how his nearness was affecting her? Would he know how much she wanted to drag him into the next room, strip him down to his skin and make mad, passionate love to him? The soft light glowing from a nightstand wrapped them in an intimate environment, designed for honeymooners or couples looking for a sexy escape.

Three years should be long enough to get over the abuse she'd suffered at the hands of her ex-husband. Three years of learning to be strong and to trust her instincts. And her instincts were telling her she could trust Sting Ray. He might be a bad-ass SEAL, but he wouldn't hurt her. Not intentionally.

So, what was holding her back from making

her move? Why were her hands and knees shaking so much she could barely control them? She wasn't a virgin about to make love for the first time. Hell, she wasn't even sure the SEAL liked her that much. What if he didn't want to make love to her? Butterflies flittered inside her belly.

"Hey." He touched his finger beneath her chin and urged her to look at him. "What's wrong?"

She stared into those incredibly blue eyes and shook her head, words refusing to voice what she was feeling. All the newfound confidence she'd worked so hard to gain over the past three years disappeared in a second.

"What are you afraid of, darling Lilly?"

"Nothing…everything," she whispered. He'd called her darling. What did that mean?

"I won't hurt you, like he did." He brushed a kiss across her forehead. "In fact, you can have the bed. I'll take the couch." He lowered his mouth toward hers, hovering a breath away. "Oh, babe, you don't have to be afraid of me."

Lilly's lungs seized and held. She willed him to finish the kiss he was so close to giving. *Please. Kiss me.* She closed her eyes and waited, her lips tingling in anticipation.

He sighed, his breath fanning across her mouth, warm and sexy. "You should go before I do something we'll both regret." Then he straightened, turned her around and gave her a gentle push toward the bedroom.

110

No. No. No. This wasn't what she'd had in mind. She wanted him to sleep with her, to hold her through the night, and make love to her.

She took two steps and almost turned around, but fear of rejection wouldn't let her.

"I want to get a shower after you're done in the bathroom," he said, his voice low and sexy.

Lilly swallowed hard to ease the lump in her throat that was choking the crap out of her vocal cords. "You should go first," she said without turning around. "I can wait."

"Are you sure? You could be fast asleep by the time I'm through."

"I want to…" She looked left then right, her gaze landing on the television. "I want to catch up on the news."

"Okay. I'll only be five minutes."

She nodded, without looking around at him.

Her pulse raced, and she rubbed clammy hands against her sides. She knew what she wanted to do. It was a big step for her. One she hadn't considered making again in her lifetime. But three years had taught her to reach for her dreams and desires.

Her most immediate desire walked past her and disappeared into the bathroom, closing the door behind him.

Lilly waited a minute before moving. Then she tiptoed to the bathroom door, leaned her ear against it and waited for the sound of the water running in the shower.

As soon as the first drops fell, she sprang

into action, stripping out of the clothes she'd been wearing since early that morning. When she was down to her underwear, she hesitated. What if he didn't want her?

Her chin rose. She'd accept it and move on. Rejection hurt but she wouldn't die. She hadn't died of the bruises and black eyes. Nor had she given up when her ex had broken her nose and dislocated her shoulder. Rejection would hurt her pride, but not her body.

If she'd learned one thing from her previous marriage and divorce, if you didn't go after what you wanted, you lived with regret.

She hadn't come this far to give up. It didn't mean a lifetime commitment, and she wouldn't ask for anything in return.

Taking a deep breath, she shucked her panties and bra, twisted the doorknob and entered the bathroom.

The outline of Sting Ray's body behind the curtain caused Lilly's blood to burn through her veins. Before she could chicken out, she slid the curtain to the side and stepped into the shower behind Sting Ray.

He stood beneath the spray, eyes closed, his back to her, rinsing suds from his hair and face.

Now that she was there, what should she do? She grabbed the bar of soap and lathered it by rolling it between her fingers and then, with shaking hands, she reached for him.

As soon as she touched his body, the world exploded around her.

"What the hell?" Sting Ray spun, grabbed her hands and shoved her up against the cold hard tiles, pressing his chest against hers, trapping her against the wall. He blinked to clear the soap and water from his eyes.

When he finally realized it was her, he leaned his head back and let go of a long hard breath. "Holy shit, Lilly, I could have killed you."

Chapter Ten

Sting Ray drew a ragged breath, willing his pulse to slow.

"I'm sorry," Lilly said, her body trembling from head to toe, her arms crushed between their bodies. "I shouldn't have...I just...I shouldn't have..." She glanced away, a rosy hue climbing up her neck and blossoming in her cheeks.

God, she was beautiful, naked and pressed against his body. What sweet hell was this?
"Oh, darlin', you can't sneak up on me like that. If I'm attacked, I'm trained to kill."

"I didn't mean to scare you. I thought..." She laughed, the sound strangled in her throat. "I guess I wasn't really thinking." Her gaze dropped to somewhere around the base of his throat, refusing to look him in the eye. "If you'll let me go, I'll go into the other room and bury my head under a pillow."

He fought the desire to laugh. Her embarrassment made her that much more endearing. "Why?" He eased her down the tile to stand on her own feet.

She snorted. "Because I've never been more mortified in my life and I should bury my head in a pillow until such a time as we forget this ever happened."

"No." He brushed a strand of her hair off

her cheek. "Why did you come in here?"

With a lopsided smile, she shrugged. "I needed a shower?"

"And it couldn't wait?" Amused, he tucked the strand of hair behind her ear.

She huffed out a breath. "What do you want me to say? That I wanted to make love to you? That I've been thinking about it practically since the moment we met? Fine. I'll say it. I want to feel you inside me. I've been thinking about getting naked with you since I first saw you. But it doesn't mean you have to do anything." She crossed her arms over her breasts. "You might not even like me. But, I'm a big girl. I can handle rejection—"

Sting Ray couldn't get a word in edgewise, so he covered her mouth with his to stem the flow of her words. When nothing but the sound of water hitting the tub and curtain could be heard, he sank into her, tracing her lips with the tip of his tongue until she opened to him. Thrusting through, he caressed and stroked, tasting the magic that was Lilly.

For every one of his thrusts, she gave back. She locked her arms around his neck and pressed her breasts to his chest.

Sting Ray couldn't believe she was in the shower with him, her naked body rubbing against this. If he wasn't careful, he'd throw caution to the wind and make love to her without protection. He broke the kiss and leaned back enough to look down into her face.

Her eyelids drooped halfway down, and her lips were swollen from their kiss.

"What do you want from me, Lilly?" he asked, his body aching to make her his.

She looked straight into his eyes and said, "I want to make love with you."

He groaned. "Just that simple?"

She nodded. "No strings. No promises. Just make love with me." Her brows drew together. "Unless you don't want to. I mean, I don't even know whether or not you like me or what you see."

"Are you kidding?" He leaned into her, the rock-hard evidence of his desire pressing against her belly. "You're making me crazy. I've wanted you since I met you, too."

She shook her head. "Even when I was so rude to you?"

"I was rude first. You put me in my place, and I think that's when I started fanaticizing about you being naked." He set her back from him and raked his gaze over the length of her. "My fantasies don't even come close to reality."

Her cheeks turned an even deeper shade of pink. "Better or worse?"

"Oh, sweetheart, so much better." He bent, cupped her ass, lifted her off her feet again and wrapped her legs around his waist, his shaft pressing against her entrance. "But I can't make love to you."

Her eyes widened. "No?"

"Yet," he added, with a smile. "We need

protection."

"Oh, yeah…that." She curled her arms around his neck and pressed a kiss to his temple. "Tell me you're a good Boy Scout and always come prepared."

"I'm a good Boy Scout, and I always come prepared." He winced. "At least I think I do." He tipped his head. "I need to check in my wallet."

"Then by all means, check." She wiggled to get down and stood on her own feet.

"Be right back." As soon as he stepped out of the bathtub, Sting Ray dove for his jeans pocket and thumbed through his wallet until he found what he was looking for. Two shiny new condom packets. He kissed the packets, swept the shower curtain back and climb back in.

Lilly stood beneath the spray, her head tilted back, rinsing shampoo from her shoulder-length hair. She'd raised her arms above her head, exposing the beauty of her body to him.

He stared for a moment, taking all of her in, from the rounded globes of her breasts to the swell of her hips. She was gorgeous. Water and suds sluiced off the tips of her perky nipples and down her torso to the tuft of dark-blond hair covering her sex.

Sting Ray's cock twitched, and it was all he could do not to grab her and drive himself deep inside her. He counted to five, willing himself to slow down, take his time and bring her along with him before he came inside her.

She lifted her head and blinked her eyes

open. A smile spread across her lips. "You found one?"

"Two." He placed the packets on the soap dish and then closed the distance between them. "Anyone ever tell you you're sexy as hell?"

She shook her head. "Not until you."

"Then let me remedy that gross oversight. You're sexy as hell." He traced a finger from her temple, over her cheek and across to her lips.

She kissed it and sucked it into her mouth, nipping the tip.

His cock swelled even tighter, eager to plunge deep inside her. He replaced his finger with his lips, tracing the same line from her temple to her lips, claiming her mouth in a deep, soul-defining kiss that left him breathless and wanting more. He lathered the soap and ran his sudsy hands over her shoulders and collarbones and lower to her bouncy breasts. He circled them twice before capturing the nipples between his thumbs and forefingers, tweaking them until they puckered into tight little beads. Too tempted to resist, he bent to suck one of those rosy buds between his lips, rolling it with his tongue.

Lilly arched her back, pressing the breast deeper into his mouth. A moan rose from her throat, echoing against the shower walls.

Sting Ray straightened, tracing his fingers down her breasts and torso to the triangle of hair over her sex. He cupped her, fingering her entrance. He wanted so much more, but not here. Guiding her beneath the water, he rinsed off all the soap, exploring her with his hands as he smoothed them over her body. When they were both clean and soap-free, he switched off the water, lifted Lilly out of the tub and toweled her dry.

She returned the favor, stopping long enough to tongue his nipples, stroke his shaft and roll his balls between her fingers.

No longer able to hold back, he scooped her into his arms and strode for the bed.

Gently laying her on the mattress, he stood back for a moment, dragging in deep, calming breaths.

Lying against the pillows, she crossed one arm over her breasts and the other hand covered her sex. "Why did you stop?"

"I want to remember you like this." He dragged his gaze over every inch of her from the tip of her damp head to the pale pink of her toenail polish. "You're absolutely beautiful."

She laughed, her cheeks filling with color. "Whatever. I'm too chubby."

"No." He pulled her arm from over her breasts and lifted the hand shielding her sex. "Don't you let anyone tell you that. You're perfect just the way you are."

She tugged his hand. "I want you," she said. "Inside me. Now." Lilly parted her legs and drew him onto the bed between them.

"You're not ready," he said, dropping down to press a kiss to each nipple.

"Oh, yes, I am." She ran one of her hands

down to the apex of her thighs and fingered her entrance. "So wet and ready."

"I want you to come with me." He trailed kisses down her torso, thrusting his tongue into her belly button and licking his way downward.

When he parted her folds, she sucked in a breath and held it.

One flick of his tongue across her clit made her expel a gasp and draw up her knees. He flicked her again, tapping the strip of flesh, tonguing her until she dug her heels into the mattress and raised her hips, thrusting herself upward.

Sting Ray had her where he wanted her. Pressing a finger to her entrance he swirled in her juices, added another finger and still another, stretching her, fucking her with his hand.

He increased the intensity of his assault on her clit, tonguing and flicking, swirling until she threaded her fingers into his hair and held him down there. Her body tensed, and she rocked her hips.

Now. He had to have her now.

With one last flick over her nubbin of flesh, Sting Ray climbed up her body and then rose up on his knees.

Damn it, he'd left the condoms in the shower.

"Looking for these?" Lilly held up the foil packets with a smile.

"I think I love you." He kissed her lips, grabbed one of the packets, tore it open and rolled it over his engorged staff. Then he settled himself between her legs, pressed his cock to her entrance and paused. He couldn't go too fast, or he'd blow his wad far too quickly. This woman had him so tightly wound, he couldn't think straight. He only wanted to fuck her until he'd used up all his strength.

Steady now. Sting Ray eased into her, careful not to hurt her.

She curled her fingers around his buttocks, tightened her hold and slammed him home.

"Oh sweet Jesus," he moaned, drew out halfway and thrust back in all the way to the hilt. His balls slapped against her ass.

She cloaked him, her channel squeezing him so snugly, he could barely think. All his blood swelled into his dick, making him so thick and hard, he could have used it to drive nails into concrete.

Lilly guided him in and out, until he took over the rhythm, driving into her, again and again. She threw back her head and dug her heels into the mattress, meeting his every thrust. Then she tensed and sank her fingers into his buttocks, crying out his name. Her body shuddered and warm liquid cloaked his cock.

Sting Ray rocketed to the heavens so fast he could barely catch his breath. He thrust one last time, burying himself inside her, his dick throbbing against her channel for the next five minutes. When at last he drifted back to earth, he lay for a long time contemplating the possibilities of dating a woman long distance. He rolled them both to the side, without losing their intimate connection.

"Incredible," he murmured.

"Yes, it was," she agreed.

He held her in his arms, loving the way she fit against him. He inhaled the scent of her, memorizing the details of her face, her skin, the way her lashes lay like dark crescents against her cheeks. This woman could easily capture a man's heart and hold it for eternity. "Lily, we need to talk."

Snuggling close, she pressed her lips to his skin. "Talk," she murmured, her voice thick. Soon her breathing grew more regular as she drifted off to sleep.

So much for talking.

For a long time, Sting Ray lay, staring up at the ceiling, trying to determine where they would go from here. Lilly deserved so much more than what he could give. His job required him to be away more than he was home.

Hell, he'd only known her a few hours. Why was he thinking long-term? Not to mention, he might not be the kind of guy Lilly needed. With Uncle Fred as an example of how *not* to show affection, Sting Ray wasn't so sure he could be any more than he was. What did he know about treating a woman right?

He lay awake well into the night, turning over his options until they were tangled and confused. Bottom line was they were two completely different people with careers that would keep them apart. Anything long-term was out of the question.

Hadn't Lilly said, *No strings. No Commitment?*

Well, hell. What if he wanted more?

Chapter Eleven

Lilly woke to light streaming through a window and across her face. She opened her eyes and closed them again quickly, blinded by the morning sun. Raising a hand, she shaded her face and tried again, at first confused by the white lace curtains and the antique furniture. Then memories flooded in, and she remembered where she was and with whom she'd slept the night before.

Heat swarmed up her neck into her cheeks. She rolled to her side expecting to see a big, handsome SEAL beside her, but found an empty pillow with a dent in it. At least it proved to her the night before hadn't been a wet dream but a sexy reality.

So, where was he?

After a big satisfying stretch, Lilly rose from the bed, wrapped a sheet around her and went in search of her missing lover.

The bathroom and sitting room were as empty of the SEAL's presence as the bedroom.

Lilly stood in the middle of the room frowning. Where had he gone? All her previous insecurities rushed in at her from all sides. God, had he thought she sucked in bed and didn't have the heart to tell her? She paced the room, almost tripping over the sheet.

No. He'd said she was incredible. He'd even said he could be in love with her when she'd held up the condoms he'd left in the bathroom.

A key scraped inside the door lock.

Lilly ran for the bathroom, grabbing her clothes as she went.

Once inside, she shut the door and leaned against it to catch her breath and get a grip on her racing heart.

"Lilly?" Sting Ray called out.

"In here," she responded, running a damp rag over her body before throwing on her clothes from the day before. "Where were you?" Did that sound needy? She didn't want to come across as needy and clingy. Men didn't like that. Nor did she like men who were clingy, or worse, controlling. She was the only one in control of her destiny.

Then why was her every emotion that morning hinging on Sting Ray's morning-after response to their lovemaking?

Once dressed, she glanced in the mirror and winced. She'd gone to bed the night before with wet hair. It now stuck out in all directions, making her look like the bride of Frankenstein. She grabbed her brush and yanked out the tangles, but nothing short of twenty minutes with her flat iron would fix the damage. She tucked the crinkled strands behind her ears and pasted a smile on her face. *Fake it until you feel it. You are a confident woman. Repeat after me…*

Lilly stepped out of the bathroom and

inhaled the permeating scent of coffee and fresh donuts.

"I brought breakfast." He held up the cup of coffee he'd been sipping on and waved it toward the tray on the small dining table. "I wasn't sure you liked coffee, so I brought an additional cup of hot water and a selection of teabags and cocoa mix."

"Perfect. I love a good cup of hot tea on a cold morning, and hot cocoa is always welcome." She grimaced. "Though I love the smell of coffee, I don't care for the flavor."

"Good. That gives me two cups to get me going." He lifted a donut from the paper plate on the tray. "I hope donuts are okay for breakfast."

"They aren't good for my waistline, but I love them." She plopped a teabag into the cup of hot water and selected a donut, wondering if he would mention last night's mattress action. She'd be quite all right if he didn't. But then again, her ego needed some feedback.

After consuming an entire donut and half a cup of tea, she asked, "Hear anything from Hank?"

Sting Ray nodded. "He's on the way. The DEA guy has been in touch with his sources and with Yasmin's CIA counterparts. They have a couple of names of people on their watch list who could be our terrorist." He'd polished off the last of his donut when a knock sounded at the door. "That will be Hank and the DEA rep." He wiped his fingers on a napkin and crossed to the door.

Hank and Bear entered with Faulkner behind them.

Bear gave Lilly a narrowed glance, opened his mouth as if to say something and clamped it shut.

Lilly's cheeks heated. Did her big brother know what she and Sting Ray had been up to the night before? She wasn't about to ask.

Faulkner took a seat at the table and opened a laptop. "We got a hit on two potential suspects. Both Americans. Each have a connection to the Ethiopian Prince Yohannis. They also have been seen with Prince Khalid's servant Rashad on several occasions in Riyadh."

Lilly and Sting Ray moved closer and leaned over Faulkner's back to stare down at the monitor.

Faulkner tapped the keys, and a photo filled the screen. A white man with sandy-blond hair and a beard sat across a café table from a black man in a dark business suit. Unfortunately, the photo was grainy, and the man's features were blurred. Faulkner pointed to the black man. "That's Prince Yohannis. The man across from him was identified as Thomas Blackstone, former US Army Special Forces. He spent time training Ethiopian military as a force multiplier. On his last mission, his wife had an affair and filed for divorce. He got slapped with the paperwork when he returned from Africa. She demanded alimony and took the kids to another state to be closer to her mother."

Lilly's lips thinned. "Nice homecoming."

"Possible motivation," Hank commented.

Faulkner continued. "Blackstone retired from the Army and went to work as a contractor out of Djibouti."

"Giving him access to the Ethiopian prince," Sting Ray concluded.

With a nod, Faulkner flipped to the next photo of Blackstone standing beside a limousine on a busy street shaking hands with a man in a white robe and the checkered headdress of the House of Saud. "Blackstone and Rashad in Riyadh. The CIA contact there said Blackstone had met with Rashad on a couple other occasions prior to the mission to recover the vials of virus. They hadn't put these meetings together with the sale of biological weapons until the SEALs uncovered the plot to kill Prince Khalid, and Rashad's part in that plan."

The next photo was of Blackstone in uniform, hair cut high and tight, face clean-shaven, and his blue eyes steely cold.

A chill slithered down Lilly's back. "Not the huggable type."

Tapping a key, Faulkner brought up a photo of a man with dark hair and dark eyes.

Lilly leaned closer. The bartender had described a man with dark hair and eyes. Could this be the man with the scorpion tattoo who'd sat with Fred at the bar?

He stood alone on a crowded street. The photographer had zoomed in on the man, blurring out the others in the photo. He had on a dark jacket and dark pants and appeared to be staring at something in the distance.

"Who is he?"

"Troy Burton. He was also seen with Prince Yohannis in Ethiopia and Rashad in Saudi." Faulkner brought up two more photos, side by side, of a man with dark hair walking with Prince Yohannis on a city street. The other was the back of a dark-haired man talking to Rashad.

"Can you tell if he has a tattoo on his arm?" Lilly asked.

"Sorry." Faulkner shook his head. "Both pictures aren't at an angle to tell."

"Troy Burton." Sting Ray faced Hank. "Can we check flight schedules into Bozeman for either of these men's names?"

Hank nodded. "Already on it. Yasmin's contacts in the CIA are searching flight records and credit card companies. We also have to consider they might be using fake identification."

Lilly clenched her fists. "Is that all we have?"

Hank nodded. "Wish it was more, but it's a start. I also asked the news station for copies of the drone videos from yesterday, hoping they were recording during the PETA parade at the time Yasmin was tagged."

"Good. Let us know what you find," Sting Ray said.

Faulkner stood, folded his laptop and tucked it under his arm. "I'll be out and about, looking for these guys. In the meantime, good luck." Faulkner left the room.

Hank and Bear walked to the door.

Bear turned back, his gaze capturing Lilly's. "Let me know if you get into any trouble." His glance moved to Sting Ray and narrowed. "Or just need a big brother to step in."

Lilly's lips twitched as she fought to keep from laughing at her brother's veiled threat. "I'm okay. But it's nice to know you're around."

He nodded and pinned Sting Ray with a stare. "You be sure to take care of my sister."

The *Or else* wasn't spoken but resonated in the room, loud and clear.

Hank and Bear left the room, closing the door behind them.

"Okay." Lilly clapped her hands together. "All we can do is keep looking."

"That's right." Sting Ray held out his hand.

Lilly placed hers in his, her heart fluttering against her ribs.

Sting Ray pulled her into his arms and tipped her chin upward. "I don't think I've actually said good morning to you."

Her cheeks heated. "You disappeared before I woke." She could have kicked herself for the accusatory whine in her tone.

"I know. I wanted to stay until you woke, but my belly was rumbling, and I figured you'd be hungry too, after all the exercise we got last night."

Her pulse pounded in her veins, sending heat burning throughout her body. "I love donuts." She regretted the inanity of her statement but was at a loss for words with his blue gaze boring down into hers.

He bent, touching his lips to hers. "Good morning, beautiful," he breathed into her mouth before claiming her. For a long, breath-stealing moment, he kissed her, his tongue tangling with hers. The sweetness of the sugary donuts was nothing compared to the purity of his kiss.

When at last he raised his head, he leaned his forehead to hers. "What are we doing?"

She laughed. "I don't know. None of this makes any sense."

"*You're* telling *me*. We've known each other for the grand total of maybe twenty-four hours, and already I don't like you out of my sight for a second."

Lilly smiled. "Imagine how I felt waking up alone in the bed."

He kissed her again—short, deep and with feeling. "I'm sorry. That shouldn't have happened."

"I thought you might have regrets," she whispered.

"No way." He hugged her to him and rested his cheek against hers. "I just can't see how anything between us could possibly work."

Lilly's chest contracted. She knew the truth of what he said, but her heart didn't want to hear it. She swallowed hard and forced out, "What did I tell you before we started?"

He pressed his lips to her temple. "No strings. No commitment." Sting Ray leaned back.

"I thought I was okay with that, but now I'm not so sure."

She wanted to shout, *Me, too!* Instead, she clamped her lips shut and gave a pathetic excuse for a smile. "We should get back to work."

"I don't feel like we're any closer, even with names to go by." Sting Ray kissed her forehead and stepped back. "It's a new day. We need to get out and see what we can find."

"You're right."

"And when this is all over, we need to talk."

"About what?" She glanced up at him.

"I don't know. I'm not very good at this, but maybe we could go on a date."

"Why?" She shrugged, filled with a strange mixture of joy at the thought he wanted to see her again and a pragmatic realization that anything between them would never work. "By the time we find the guy terrorizing you and your team, my vacation will be over. I'll go back to work in Atlanta and you'll go back to..." She planted a fist on her hip. "Just where is it you work out of?"

He smiled. "Little Creek, Virginia. If we go out on a date, you can ask all the questions you want. I might not be able to answer all of them, especially if it's classified, but I'll do the best I can."

"You don't get it, do you?"

"Get what? That I'm attracted to you and don't want this to end after a few short days?" He pulled her back into his arms. "If that's what you're talking about, then yeah, I don't get it.

There has to be a way."

She shook her head. "You're a hopeless romantic."

Sting Ray's eyes opened wide. "Me?" He stared at her as if she'd lost her mind. "How can I be a hopeless romantic? I don't have the background. My uncle barely showed an ounce of affection. My parents died before I learned to date. If you give me a chance, you could teach me to be a romantic. But I'm not one, now. I've never been good at this guy-girl mating dance."

She smacked her palm against his chest. "The hell you aren't. Last night was proof of that." Lilly held up her hand. If they stayed in the room much longer, she'd be dragging him back to the bed. An entire community relied on them to catch the terrorist before he unleashed the virus on everyone. "As much as I'd like to stay and make love, we have a job to do."

Before she could change her mind, she marched out the door and down the steps to the SUV. It was hard walking away from him, but she did it. She might as well get some practice in now. When it was all said and done, she'd be kissing him goodbye and going back to her life. Alone.

Chapter Twelve

Sting Ray fought hard to keep from going after Lilly, tossing her over his shoulder and carrying her back up the stairs to toss her in the middle of the king-sized bed. As it was, his jeans were so tight he had difficulty descending the stairs to join Lilly by the SUV. He managed, but it was painful.

"Are we driving or walking?" she asked.

"Depends on where we're going." He glanced up and down the street. "Let's look around and see who might have some security cameras. Maybe there's footage close to the time my uncle was in town."

"Good idea. I hope they get the news drone footage soon. I'd like to know if they caught an image of the guy who darted Yasmin."

Sting Ray kept Lilly on the inside of the sidewalk, away from the street. Considering Yasmin had been shot from a home lining the main drag, Sting Ray wasn't certain having her on the inside was the right thing to do. Hell, now that they were more than partners in solving a mystery, he was worried the terrorist would target her. "Lilly, it might be a good idea to cool it on anything between me and you."

"What?" She ground to a halt and shot an angry glance at him. "First you want a date, and now you don't want anything to do with me?"

"I don't want anyone to think we have anything between us." He shook his head. "This isn't coming out right. I told you I sucked at this." He looked at anything but her to avoid bringing her back into his embrace and showing everyone in town how he felt about this woman. "If the terrorist is targeting people we care about, he'll target you next."

Her anger drained from her face, and she sighed. "Do you get the feeling we weren't meant to be?"

"Not really." He started walking. "I actually think we *were* meant to be, just not now. Not when being associated with me puts people in danger."

"Excuse me," a female voice called out from across the street.

Sting Ray glanced up to see a young woman emerge from a florist's shop.

"Are you Mr. Thompson's nephew?" She carried a single pink rose in her hand.

Sting Ray nodded. "I am." He altered course, steering Lilly with him to meet the woman before she crossed the street. "Why do you ask?"

"I don't know what to do with this." She held up the long-stemmed pink rose. "And the one from yesterday. Is your uncle okay?"

"He's sick in the hospital," Sting Ray replied.

The woman's brows puckered. "Oh. I'm sorry to hear that. I hope he gets well soon."

"Me too." He nodded toward the flower.

"What does the rose have to do with my uncle?"

She smiled. "He has a standing order for a single pink rose every day."

"How long has that been going on?" he asked.

"My boss said, he's been here every day for the past six years." The woman sighed. "It's so romantic. He takes the rose to the cemetery. He must have loved his wife very much."

Sting Ray's gut lurched. Had he ever known his uncle? The old man had rarely gone to town when Sting Ray lived there. He certainly didn't buy flowers. "He wasn't married," Sting Ray said, his tone flat.

The young girl's brows dipped. "Really? I thought he was." She shook herself and held out the rose. "Since he's not here, would you give this to him? I have to get back to work."

Sting Ray took the rose.

"Miss." Lilly stepped forward. "Was Mr. Thompson here two days ago?"

The woman's brow wrinkled. "Of course. He never missed a day until yesterday. He usually comes in around four in the afternoon." Then she was gone, hurrying back to the shop.

Sting Ray glanced up at the eaves of the buildings surrounding the flower shop. "If he was at the florist at four and the bar before that, he would have walked this way." He followed the sidewalk, looking over the doors for any signs of security cameras. "Why would anyone need a security camera here? They leave their doors unlocked, for Pete's sake."

"What's that?" Lilly pointed to what looked like just what they were looking for, a single security camera positioned over the door of the liquor store. "Let's check it out."

Sting Ray opened the door for her and followed her inside, his heartbeat kicking up a notch. Would they finally get a break in this case? It all hinged on the liquor storeowner keeping his system up to date.

No one was behind the counter at the front of the store. "Can I help you find something?" a voice called out from the rear of the building.

"Actually, yes." Lilly turned on a mega-watt smile that made Sting Ray's heart flip with a pang of jealousy. "I'm Lilly Parker, and this is my boyfriend, Ray Thompson." She stuck out her hand.

The man shook her hand and let go. "Bob Jones. What is it you need?" He shook Sting Ray's hand and turned back to Lilly.

"We're retracing the steps of Ray's uncle, trying to find out what he might have gotten into to that made him sick. We think he passed by your store two days ago around 3:30 in the afternoon. We noticed you have a security camera outside. Does it work?"

The man nodded. "It sure does. My son installed it last week as a birthday gift. He thought I might have fun fooling with it." He snorted. "Like I have spare time. You're welcome to look through the archives. I'll show you what he showed me, but from there, you're on your own."

"Thank you." Lilly flashed her smile again, and the man stumbled over an empty box, trying to get free of his stock.

His cheeks flushed red. "Follow me."

Lilly shot a grin back at Sting Ray.

He felt like the storeowner and nearly tripped over his own feet. Lilly had a beautiful smile, a beautiful body and a big heart. Any man would be lucky to have her as his girlfriend or wife.

Bob led them to a small office in the back with a computer perched in the middle of an old metal desk. He sat for a few minutes, fiddling with the keyboard. He finally brought up a screen with an image of the front of the store and people walking by. "This is what's happening now." He showed Lilly how to look through the archives, and then stood to allow her to sit in the seat.

The bell over the front door rang.

"I have customers," he said. "Let me know if you get stuck. I'm not sure I can help, but then again, maybe I can."

"Thank you, Mr. Jones." Lilly went to work scrolling through the archives until she arrived at the 3:00pm on the day Sting Ray's uncle got sick. "I'll run it through at two times the speed so we can go faster."

She sped through the first fifteen minutes and slowed as the recording neared 3:45.

Sting Ray didn't see his uncle until 3:48. "There." Fred Thompson passed the liquor store and kept walking like a man on a mission, his strong jaw tight, his focus on the sidewalk ahead of him. Sting Ray's chest tightened. This was the uncle he remembered. The strong, determined man who'd raised him, not the sick old guy in the hospital. Anger roiled in his belly.

A second later, a man with dark hair and wearing a dark jacket walked up behind Fred. He turned his head toward the street as he passed the camera. All the camera caught was the back of the man's head, not his face. He reached out and patted Fred on the shoulder close to the neck, like an old friend. Just as they stepped out of view of the camera, the man dropped his hand.

Lilly paused the video. "What's that?" she exclaimed.

"Can you zoom in?" Sting Ray leaned closer.

She worked with the controls and enlarged the area around Fred's neck.

Sting Ray's gut knotted. "Looks like the dart used on Yasmin."

"Bastard," Lilly muttered. She zoomed back out, backed up the video and played through the scene again. "Watch there." She pointed at the screen as the man dropped his arm. She slowed the video until it moved frame by frame. Before the men moved out of the view, they could see his arm and the bare skin of his wrist with the distinct marking of a scorpion tattoo.

Sting Ray sagged in disappointment. "Damn. We didn't see his face."

"He had dark hair and a dark jacket."

"Like half of the cowboys in Eagle Rock

right now. Without a face to recognize, we have no more to go on than we started with."

Lilly fast-forwarded the video hoping to catch the man on his return trip along the sidewalk, but he didn't come back the way he went. She stood and stretched. "We should go check the cemetery and see if it gives us any clues."

"Wouldn't hurt." Sting Ray lifted the rose. Perhaps they'd find out who his uncle visited, revealing yet another facet of his uncle's life he hadn't shared with his nephew.

They walked back to the SUV. Sting Ray handed the rose to Lilly, and drove to the cemetery on the opposite edge of town from the rodeo. When he got out of the SUV, he could hear the loudspeaker, even at that distance.

"Any idea who your uncle was visiting here?" Lilly asked as she joined him at the cemetery gate.

"Not a clue. My parents were cremated, their ashes spread over the ocean. Their parents weren't buried here, either."

"We should probably look for some faded roses like this one. To make this go faster, I'll take the right, you can take the left." Lilly took off to the right.

Sting Ray swung left and walked down one long row of graves marked by old tombstones. He moved from row to row, without finding anything.

"Hey. I found it," Lilly called out. She stood at the far corner beneath the shade of a maple tree, staring down.

Sting Ray joined her and read the name on the marker. "Eileen Hughes. That's Charlie's wife."

"Interesting." Lilly laid the rose beside one whose petals had faded. "Do you think he made a promise to Charlie to put flowers on his wife's grave?"

"I don't know." Hell, he didn't know much about his uncle. But the man wasn't quite as taciturn as he'd always thought. In fact, the man had a heart buried in all the silence. He played checkers with an old friend who was suffering from dementia and fixed the guy's porch step. "I don't know what it means, but I know someone who might. It probably has nothing to do with this case, but I feel the need to know." He headed for the SUV and held the door for Lilly.

Lilly smiled. "I understand. Who did you have in mind?"

"The biggest gossip in town." He shook his head. "I should have thought of her before."

"Where is she?"

"At the sheriff's office. She's the dispatcher."

"Perfect place for gathering information."

"Yeah." He closed Lilly's door, and got into the driver's side.

It only took a few minutes to reach the sheriff's office. The sheriff was out patrolling the rodeo, keeping the peace and looking for someone spreading a virus. The deputy behind the desk waved them through to the dispatcher's office.

"Ray Thompson? Is that you?" A petite, gray-haired woman pulled off her headset and engulfed him in a hug. "I heard about your uncle. I wasn't on duty at the time, but they told me what happened. I hope he's doing better."

"Ms. Pennington, you're a sight for sore eyes." He hugged her back. "As far as I know, my uncle is holding his own." He needed to go by and visit Fred as soon as he had a chance. Hopefully, he'd be out of quarantine in a few days. "I hope you can help me."

"Sure." She stood back, planting her hands on her narrow hips. "Shoot."

"My uncle took a rose to Eileen Hughes's grave every day for the past six years? Do you know what that's all about?"

Ms. Pennington sighed. "Oh, I'm sure Fred would be mad at me for telling you, but it might help you to understand him better. Hell, he should have told you himself, but he's so private about his life."

"No kidding," Sting Ray said and waited for the woman to go on.

"Back before you came to live with him, your uncle was good friends with Charlie Hughes. They played poker together, went on hunting trips and fished whenever they had a chance. One day, a pretty young woman moved here from Kalispell to teach at the school. Both Charlie and Fred fell in love with her."

"Eileen?"

142

The older woman sighed. "Yes. It was sad, really. Fred asked me to help him pick out an engagement ring. While we were away in Bozeman doing that, Charlie asked Eileen to marry him first. I think Eileen loved both of them. When Fred found out Charlie had asked her to marry him, he stepped out of the way of his friend. He didn't force Eileen to make the choice, because he never asked her himself." Ms. Pennington poked a finger at Sting Ray. "If you ask me, he should have given her the choice, and asked. I think she would have married him instead of Charlie."

Lilly sighed. "That's so sad."

"Yeah, I think it's why your uncle moved out of town into that raggedy old cabin in the backwoods. For the longest time, he didn't come into town. When he'd heard Eileen had passed away, he came back for her funeral and was there for his old friend. Since then, he's been a regular back in town, and he started leaving roses on Eileen's grave. With Charlie's memory going, I guess Fred figured it wouldn't hurt."

"Thanks." Sting Ray turned to go.

Ms. Pennington touched his arm. "Your uncle is a good man. He doesn't always show it. But he's a good man. And he was so proud of you joining the Navy."

Sting Ray walked out of the sheriff's office, his head spinning. He never really knew his uncle. The man who'd had a hard time showing his emotion was a man nursing a broken heart.

Lilly laid her hand on his arm. "Are you all right?"

He nodded. "I need to visit my uncle."

Chapter Thirteen

Lilly nodded and climbed into the SUV. She could tell Sting Ray was chewing on the information they'd received about his uncle.

"Did you know any of that about your uncle?" she asked.

Sting Ray's hands tightened on the steering wheel until his fingers turned white. "No. I'm beginning to think I never really knew my uncle at all."

"Hopefully, he'll recover, and you two can get to know each other better."

"He *will* recover."

Thirty minutes later, they arrived at the hospital in Bozeman. Lilly had called ahead to let the others know they were coming.

Irish and Claire met them in the front lobby.

"Big Bird?" Sting Ray asked.

Claire shook her head. "He chose to be quarantined with Yasmin. He hasn't started showing symptoms, but Yasmin is. She's pretty sick. It came on pretty fast."

"What about Uncle Fred?"

Claire shook her head.

Lilly slid her hand into Sting Ray's.

"He's hanging by a thread." Irish placed his arm around Claire.

"Has he regained consciousness?" Lilly

swallowed the lump burning at the back of her throat.

Irish's jaw tightened. "No. But we haven't given up hope."

"Nor have we." Lilly squeezed Sting Ray's hand.

He returned the pressure.

Irish motioned toward the door. "Claire and I are headed out to get something to eat. Want to join us?"

"No, thanks. I came to see my uncle." Sting Ray glanced past them toward the elevator bank.

"We'll be back in an hour or less," Claire said.

Sting Ray caught Irish's arm. "Be careful out there. He got to Yasmin. He could just as easily get to you two."

Claire smiled and hooked her arm through Irish's. "We'll be careful."

They left through the front door.

Lilly glanced out at the fading light and wondered where the day had gone. Reviewing the videos had taken a couple of hours. The visit to the cemetery and the drive to Bozeman had taken them through the afternoon. With the sun setting, the sky was turning a deep gray. She followed Sting Ray to the elevators and up to the quarantine room.

Through the glass, they watched as Big Bird stood beside Yasmin's bed, holding her hand, his face set in a worried frown.

The CIA agent lay still, her skin dark against

the stark, white sheets. Like Uncle Fred in the bed beside her, she was hooked up to an IV and an array of monitors.

Sting Ray's uncle lay like he had the first time they'd visited, still and pale.

A nurse, dressed in a protective suit moved between the two hospital beds, adjusting the sheets, fluffing the pillows and checking the IV drips.

Sting Ray tapped on the glass to get Big Bird's attention.

The Navy SEAL turned and walked toward them. He stopped and pressed his fist to the glass.

Sting Ray curled his fingers and gave the man a fist bump, the glass keeping their hands from actually touching. It was the best they could do. "How are they?" he asked.

Big Bird grimaced and looked back at Yasmin. "We'll know when they pull out of it. The staff here doesn't have any experience with the symptoms. All we can do is wait and pray."

"How about you?" Lilly inquired.

"So far, I haven't contracted the virus. But they won't clear me for a while. I could be a carrier since I've been with Yasmin since the onset of her symptoms." His eyes narrowed. "Any luck finding the bastard who's doing this?"

Sting Ray shook his head. "No."

"We pinpointed when Mr. Thompson was infected. We found a security camera that recorded the event."

Big Bird leaned closer, his eyes wide,

expectant. "Then you saw who did it."

Lilly pressed her lips together. "No. The man had his back to the camera. He's got dark hair and a scorpion tattoo on the inside of his right wrist."

"That should be easy to find," Big Bird said. "How many people have a tattoo on the inside of their wrist?"

"Unfortunately, it's getting colder," Sting Ray informed him. "People are wearing long sleeves. Unless we stop everyone on the street and ask them to roll up their sleeves, we won't see the tattoo."

Big Bird banged his fist on the glass, barely containing his frustration. "Can't we set up a road block or a checkpoint and have the sheriff's department do a hundred percent check on the people in Eagle Rock?"

"I don't think we can do that without violating civil liberties," Sting Ray said.

"Desperate times require desperate measures," Big Bird said. He turned to Lilly. "Can't you get the CDC to get more involved?"

"I'll check with my higher headquarters. They were supposed to send people in to help with the investigation." She pulled her cell phone from her pocket and backed away from the glass wall. She'd been so busy following leads all day, she'd forgotten to check in with her boss.

She dialed the number that connected with her boss's personal cell phone.

"Lilly, I was just about to call you. Has the team arrived in Eagle Rock?"

"I haven't received a call. I'm in Bozeman now."

"Their flight got delayed in Denver. I would have thought they'd have made it to Bozeman by now." He paused, and Lilly could hear beeping sounds. "I'm sending you a text with their flight information. You can check with the Bozeman airport to see if they've arrived."

Lilly ended the call with her boss and dialed the Bozeman airport. They reported the flight still on the ground in Denver, delayed due to maintenance issues. Lilly ended that call and returned to the window. "Sorry. The team they sent is stuck in Denver with plane maintenance issues."

Big Bird shook his head. "We can't let this guy get away with this." He turned toward Yasmin and muttered, "I can't lose her."

"We'll do the best we can," Lilly promised.

"Irish saw all of those villagers," Big Bird mumbled, his gaze so sad it made Lilly's heart hurt. "They all died."

Sting Ray pressed his palm to the window. "Those villagers had no modern healthcare. They didn't have access to some of the best medicines and doctors in the world. Yasmin is in good hands. She's tough. She'll make it." He prayed he was right, and that his uncle would pull through as well. The medical staff was working through the night to ensure he survived the ravages of the virus.

"Do you want us to bring you something to

eat?" Lilly asked.

Big Bird shook his head. "No. The hospital staff has been feeding me. The food is better than MREs. You two should go, get something eat and get back to work. We need answers. We need to nail that bastard."

Lilly and Sting Ray stopped at the nurse's station and got an update on Fred's status. They were keeping him in a medically-induced coma to allow his body to fight the disease. If his vital signs continued to improve, they hoped to bring him out of it the next day.

That was the most optimistic news Lilly had heard in the past two days. An hour after they'd entered, they left the quarantine area and took the elevator to the lobby. They were halfway across the tiled floor to the exit when Irish crashed through the doors, carrying Claire. "I need a doctor!" he yelled.

"Put me down," Claire said, her face pale, her eyes glassy. "I can walk."

"Like hell you can." Big Bird retained his hold on her.

Lilly hurried toward the two. "What's going on?"

Claire held up her hand. "Stay back. You don't want to get close enough to contract the virus."

"You're infected?" Sting Ray asked.

Claire nodded and rubbed the back of her neck. "I must have gotten hit on our way through the parking lot." She touched the back of her neck. "I felt a sting, but it didn't last long, and didn't hurt after the initial pain. I thought nothing of it until we were sitting in the line at the drive through, waiting to order." Her words slowed and her voice faded. "I started to feel nauseated...and...feverish." Claire went limp.

Sting Ray had run to the emergency department, returning with two orderlies and a gurney. The men wore the full protective gear, including a hood, gloves and the body suit. They took Claire from Irish's arms, laid her on the gurney and wheeled her to the elevator.

Irish followed.

Sting Ray would have gone with them, but Irish put a stop to that. "Stay here. I've already been exposed, but you two are still in the clear. It's vital you find this guy before he gets to you."

The elevator door closed.

Sting Ray turned to Lilly. "I'm worried about you."

"Me? I'm not the one infected. They are."

"Yes, but you could be next."

"And you." She laid her hand on his chest. "This is insane. We have to find him and put a stop to this madness."

Sting Ray couldn't agree more. So far, the perpetrator had succeeded in his efforts to take out the people Irish and Big Bird cared about. In the process, he'd managed to expose the two men as well. Sting Ray's uncle lay in a coma, fighting for his life. Which left Sting Ray as the last man standing. He could be the next target, unless the terrorist had figured out Lilly now meant something to him. Then he would use her to get to Sting Ray.

The lobby doors opened, and Marcus Faulkner entered. "Sting Ray, Lilly, I didn't expect to find you two here. What's going on?"

Sting Ray raised his fist and shook it, rage burning a hole in his gut. "Apparently, the terrorist is here in Bozeman."

Faulkner's eyes widened and he shot a glance around in both directions. "Why do you think that?"

"Claire was hit in the hospital parking lot an hour ago," Sting Ray explained.

"These parking lots are well-lit," Lilly said. "They probably have security cameras on every light pole. We might be able to catch the culprit, maybe even from multiple angles and actually see his face this time." Lilly looked right and left, spotted the information desk and started toward it.

Sting Ray and Faulkner fell in behind her.

Lilly got directions to the security office and headed for the elevator.

Sting Ray's phone rang, the caller ID indicating it was Hank. Stopping short of the elevator, Sting Ray held up a finger. "Wait for me." He didn't want to get into the elevator and risk being cut off. Hank might have important information they could use to solve the case and nail the culprit.

"Sting Ray, we got the video from the news channel's drone," Hank said.

"Good. Did you find anything?"

The elevator door opened. Lilly pointed to the car. "I'm going to the security office. Meet me there." Lilly entered the elevator and pressed a button.

"I'll go with her." Faulkner jumped in before the door closed.

"Wait," Sting Ray said, but the elevator was already on its way to the basement parking lot where the security office was located.

"Sting Ray, are you there?"

"I'm here, but hurry. I need to catch up to Lilly."

"We know who it is. We saw him on the video. We were able to zoom in and see him blow the dart through a regular drinking straw. We could even see the tattoo on his right wrist."

Sting Ray gripped the phone. "You got an image? You can identify him?"

"Yes. And he was right there all along. We backed up through the rodeo events as well and he was there the day your uncle was hit. He pretended to have arrived the day after, but he was there all along," Hank said.

"Damn it, Hank. Who is it?"

"The guy claiming to be from the DEA—Marcus Faulkner. He must be using some trumped-up identification. We also got prints from your SUV. The prints match up with the guy Marcus was suggesting, Thomas Blackstone."

153

"Blackstone had blond hair and blue eyes. Marcus is dark on both counts."

"Hair dye and contacts. The videos don't lie, Faulkner's our guy and I'll bet his prints match with Blackstone's." Bear and I are on our way to you."

"Fuck!" Sting Ray ran for the elevator and hit the button several times.

"What's wrong?" Hank said.

Sting Ray's heart thundered against his ribs. "Faulkner is with Lilly right now."

"We're on our way. You've got to stop him."

"I will. If he hurts one hair on her head, I'll kill him." Sting Ray shoved the phone into his pocket and raced for the stairs. He hopped over the rails and dropped to the floor below in one leap. Then he slammed through the door into the parking lot.

Chapter Fourteen

Lilly exited the elevator hellbent on getting to the security office and busting the rat-bastard who'd infected Fred, the SEALs and their ladies. The spread of the virus had to be stopped before it got out of control.

"This way," Faulkner grabbed her arm and pulled her deeper into the garage.

"But the lady at the information desk said turn right."

"I know a short cut," he said, refusing to release her arm.

Lilly dug her heels into the concrete. "No. I'm sure it's this way."

Faulkner wrapped his arm around her neck. That's when Lilly saw the tattoo on the inside of his wrist. But it was too late. He had her in a headlock.

"You!" she gasped before he cut of her air.

Lilly struggled, kicking, twisting and pulling at the arm around her throat. He was bigger, stronger and crazier than she was. He'd kill her if she didn't get away.

With no other choice and her vision blurring, Lilly let her body go limp, allowing gravity to take over.

Apparently, Faulkner wasn't expecting that. His arm loosened, and her lost his hold on her throat.

Lilly ducked her head, slipped free and dove away from him, hitting the ground with a jarring jolt. She rolled to the side and bunched her legs beneath her.

A voice called out, "Lilly!"

She almost cried with relief. "Sting Ray! Over here!"

"Move, and I'll infect you." Faulkner stood less than three feet from her. He held a drink straw to his lips, aimed at her.

"Lilly!" Sting Ray erupted from around the side of a car.

"Don't come closer!" Lilly yelled. "He's got a dart."

"Yeah, and you'll witness her getting the virus," Faulkner shouted. "Then you'll watch her die. Just like I watched all of my dreams die."

"Thomas Blackstone," Sting Ray said. "Yeah, I know who you are. You were once Special Forces, a proud solider and an honorable man."

"What did that buy me?" he snarled at Sting Ray. "A busted marriage. And she left me with debt I couldn't begin to dig my way out of."

"She did you wrong, Thomas. Don't let her bring you down to her level."

"It's too late for that. No matter what I do, I'm going to hell. I might as well take a few with me." He raised the straw to his lips.

"Wait," Sting Ray said, moving closer.

Lilly inched backward, afraid to move too fast and set Blackstone off.

"Don't do it, Thomas," Sting Ray said. "She's done nothing to hurt you."

He snorted. "No, but you have. Now you'll have the pleasure of watching her downfall."

Sting Ray took a different tactic. "Why? She means nothing to me."

Blackstone's lip curled back in a sneer. "I know what you two did. A man doesn't spend the night in a one-bedroom apartment with a woman without fucking her. Ask my ex."

"That's all it was, though," Sting Ray argued. "Ask her. She said it herself. No strings, no commitment. We just scratched an itch, and we'll part ways." Sting Ray waved toward him. "If you want to hurt me, then hurt *me*." He moved even closer.

"No. It has to be her. She was the one who ruined my life. She was the one sleeping around, while I was working to pay for her fancy clothes and shoes."

"That was your ex. Not this woman," Sting Ray insisted.

"It's all women. They're all out to bring us to our knees. Well, fuck that!" He inhaled.

Lilly bunched her muscles and launched herself to the left.

Blackstone blew a sharp blast through the straw.

Sting Ray threw himself in front of Lilly and fell to the ground.

Lilly didn't feel the sting she expected. Blackstone had missed. Her elation was short-lived as Sting Ray leaped to his feet and charged into Blackstone while the insane man reloaded his straw.

The SEAL hit the terrorist in the midsection sending both of them flying across the concrete.

Blackstone took the brunt of the crash, his back hitting hard. But he rolled to the side and pushed to his feet before Sting Ray could. He bunched his fists and swung at the SEAL, hitting him in the belly.

Sting Ray staggered backward, regained his balance and hit Blackstone in the jaw.

The man's head snapped backward and he fell to his knees.

Sting Ray hit him again with enough force to send the former soldier down for the count. Then he lifted Blackstone by the collar, cocked his arm and prepared to slam his fist into the terrorist's face again.

Lilly couldn't stand it. "Sting Ray. Stop." The man didn't deserve mercy. But Lilly couldn't let Sting Ray lose his humanity over a bottom-dwelling bastard like Blackstone. "Please."

Her voice broke through Sting Ray's rage, stilling his fist before it was unleashed yet again on Blackstone's face. "Give me one good reason I shouldn't kill him."

"It's not necessary."

"What if Uncle Fred and Yasmin die? He'll be responsible." Sting Ray held the man by the collar, his muscles bulging, his lips curled back in a feral snarl.

"If you kill him, you lose a piece of your own humanity," Lilly said.

"I've killed before."

"But you don't have to, now." She rose to her feet and stood beside him, laying a hand on his arm. "He's out cold. Let him go."

"He doesn't deserve to live," he whispered. "He almost killed you."

"But he didn't." She turned his face so that he had to look her in the eye. "I'm okay."

Blackstone bucked in his grip, reaching for Lilly.

Lilly gasped and backed away.

Sting Ray punched the man in the face and let him fall to the ground. Blackstone lay still. A security guard came running toward them. "What's going on?"

"This man tried to kill me," Lilly said.

The guard got on his radio, asking for assistance from the local police department. Soon the parking garage was filled with cop cars and uniformed officers.

Sting Ray and Lilly stood back, letting them handle the chaos.

Lilly looked up at the man who'd captured her heart and passion in such a short amount of time. Yeah, they had jobs in different states. They would probably have to make complicated arrangements to get to see each other, but none of that seemed to matter. She wanted to be with him. She wanted to get to know this man. "About that date?" she looked up at him. "When and where?"

"Soon. You name it. I don't care, so long as I'm with you," he said, but his words were slow and slurred like a man well on his way to being drunk.

Lilly looked closer at the man she suspected she was falling in love with. That's when she realized something wasn't right.

He clamped his hand to the back of his neck and swayed, his eyes appearing glassy and his face pale. "Maybe I could take a little nap...first."

Lilly pulled his hand away from his neck and noticed for the first time, the tiny dart protruding from the skin. "Damn it, Sting Ray. You could have told me he'd tagged you." She hooked her arm around his middle. "I need a gurney and a doctor. Now!"

"What about our date?" Sting Ray's legs buckled, and he would have fallen if Lilly hadn't been holding on to him.

"I'll take a rain check on that date. But you're not getting out of it. And damn it, you better remember you made a date with me when you recover from this virus." She held him up, straining against his weight. "And you damn well better come out of it alive. I want that date."

"Sweetest words ever spoken." Sting Ray's body went limp, and he melted to the ground, taking Lilly with him.

Chapter Fifteen

Sting Ray opened his eyes to a glaring white light. He closed them and moaned. He felt like he'd been hit by a truck. His head hurt, his throat ached and something might have died in his mouth. But he was awake.

He tried again, this time managing to keep his eyes open for more than a second. When he tried to move his arms, he couldn't. One seemed to be hooked up to a tangle of tubes. His gaze followed the tubes up to a couple of bags of fluid. What the hell?

Slowly, his memory trickled back to him. There'd been a virus and a guy with a straw. He'd infected Irish, Claire, Yasmin and Uncle Fred.

Sting Ray's other arm seemed to be pinned to the bed with a heavy weight. When he turned that direction, all he could see was blond hair. "Lilly?" he said, but his voice didn't work. It didn't make a sound.

She lifted her head and stared up into his eyes. "Sting Ray?" she said, her voice muffled as if coming from the end of a long tunnel.

He tried to answer, but nothing came out.

Lilly's eyes widened, and she rose to stand beside him. "Hey, darlin'. It's good to see your baby blues."

He wanted to tell her his eyes weren't baby

blue. They were steely blue. But his eyelids grew heavier until he didn't have the strength to hold them open.

Voices woke him the next time, talking loud enough he couldn't ignore them. Sting Ray puckered his lips and tried to blow a stream of air through to shush the noise.

"Ray, honey," Lilly's voice said. "Open your eyes. I know you're awake."

He struggled mightily until he managed to push his eyelids open.

A beautiful angel stared down at him.

"Did I die?" he said, his voice sounding like more of a croak than he recalled.

"No, baby. You're very much alive and you're getting better."

He closed his eyes again and sighed. "Thought I saw an angel."

Her chuckle warmed his heart and made him open his eyes again.

"Uh-huh. There she is again." He was able to focus on the room, his gaze following someone fully covered in a protective suit and hood. "Did your team get here?"

Lilly smiled down at him and lifted his hand to her lips. "They did."

"Yasmin and Claire?"

"Recovering nicely. They'll be released tomorrow."

"Irish and Big Bird?"

"Healthy as horses, and waiting for their

teammate to get well."

"Uncle Fred?"

"You're chatty for a sick man." Lilly laughed. "Fred's standing outside the quarantine room looking in. He made it."

"And is he as grumpy as ever?"

Lilly grinned. "I think he's a big teddy bear. He and I are on a first name basis, now."

"You're kidding." He closed his eyes, exhaustion leading him back to la-la land. But something wasn't quite right. He opened his eyes again and stared at Lilly. "Where's your protective suit?"

She brushed a hand over his forehead and kissed his cheek. "I'm not wearing one."

"Obviously. But you'll get sick."

"I'm willing to risk it," she said.

"Why?"

She pressed his hand to her cheek and smiled. "I wanted to be able to touch you."

His chest swelled and a tear slipped from the corner of his eye. "You're not so smart for a woman working for the CDC, you know that?"

"Hey, Rude Man. Maybe not, but I think I'm falling for a big, dumb lug of a SEAL."

Sting Ray smiled and slipped back into the darkness, his heart lighter than he'd ever dreamed. Yes, he 'd probably died and gone to heaven. And it was every bit as wonderful as he'd imagined.

Epilogue

"Sweetheart, could you get that new bottle of barbeque sauce out of the pantry?" Sting Ray called out.

"This one?" Lilly slipped through the French doors onto the back deck, weaving her way through the patio chairs to the grill.

Sting Ray bent to kiss her. "You read my mind."

"It's a good thing we stocked up. If I'd known you were inviting the entire SEAL team to dinner, I would have baked a cake." She smiled at the men lounged in chairs they'd brought themselves, their women sitting beside them or in their laps.

"When are you two going to get married?" Irish asked.

Claire sat in his lap, twirling her finger in his hair.

"I could ask the same question," Lilly shot back at Irish. She raised her brows in challenge.

Claire held up her left hand, displaying a shiny new ring. "As a matter of fact, we're getting married next month in Vegas. You're all invited to the wedding."

Irish grinned from ear to ear. "That's right. You heard the little lady. She said yes. We're getting hitched."

Yasmin rose from Big Bird's lap and leaned over Claire's hand. "That's some rock you have there. Don't let him skimp on the honeymoon, sweetie. Make him take you to a tropical island."

"Fish and Natalie," Irish nodded toward the couple, "recommended one of the cays off the coast of Belize. They say the water there is crystal clear, and it won't break the bank. We'll get to do some scuba diving and deep sea fishing. Main thing is all of you getting to Vegas for the wedding."

"And the bachelor party," Caesar Sanchez said. "Don't forget the bachelor party." He grunted when Lt. Erin McGee jabbed her elbow into his belly. "What?" he raised his hands. "You know I love you. Those strippers don't own even a little piece of my heart."

"Better keep it that way," Erin said. "I didn't risk my career for you to have you cheating on me."

"No way. You're the one for me." He dropped into a chair and pulled her into his lap, kissing her soundly.

"Gator, what about you?" Irish asked. "Can you make it?"

He glanced at his wife, the FBI agent. "How about it, Mitchell? Can we swing it?"

She ran a hand across her swollen belly. "I'm not sure they'll let me on a plane at eight months pregnant." She grimaced as the baby rolled, creating a wave across her shirt. "We'll have to wish you well from back home."

Gator shrugged. "Sorry, Irish. Mama and baby comes first."

"I wouldn't expect you to come," Claire said. "You should be sitting in a comfortable lounge chair with your feet up at that point."

"Thankfully, I'm on desk duty until after the baby's born." Mitchell chuckled. "Who would have thought I'd ever be pregnant?"

Each one of the men raised a hand, including Gator, and said, "Me."

"God, I wish men could have babies. They wouldn't be so quick to get pregnant." Mitchell shot a glance toward Claire. "Adopt. And make it a golden retriever."

Lilly smiled at all her new friends, who'd quickly become like family.

Sting Ray curled an arm around her waist and pulled her close.

She sighed and leaned into his side. "I'm glad the CDC let me hire on as a contractor. I still get some great work assignments, but the best part is getting to be with you when you're in town."

"When I leave the Navy, if you want to live in Atlanta and go back to work for them, I'd be happy to follow you."

"I don't know. I was thinking Montana might be a great place to live. We could be closer to your uncle."

Sting Ray stared down at her, his heart swelling. "You mean it? I wouldn't ask you to move to such a remote town, but I've been thinking about it a lot lately."

"I'd move there on one condition," she said.

"And that is?"

"You take me to that lake high in the mountains to fish."

"Deal." He kissed her lips and nibbled on her ear. "And I'll carry the sleeping bag. Because there's a lot more to do than fish up there under the stars with no one around."

"And when might we go?" she whispered, suddenly wishing all their friends would disappear so they could get naked.

"Hank offered to let me come to work for him whenever I'm ready."

"And are you ready?"

He growled against her cheek. "Babe, you have no idea just how ready I am."

"Sting Ray, could you quit kissing your woman?" Tuck called out. "You're burning our burgers."

Sting Ray tossed the spatula toward Tuck, swung Lilly up in his arms and marched into the house, calling out over his shoulder. "Help yourself to the food, and show yourselves out when you're done. I've got a date with a hot chick."

THE END

About the Author

ELLE JAMES also writing as MYLA JACKSON is a *New York Times* and *USA Today* Bestselling author of books including cowboys, intrigues and paranormal adventures that keep her readers on the edges of their seats. With over eighty works in a variety of sub-genres and lengths she has published with Harlequin, Samhain, Ellora's Cave, Kensington, Cleis Press, and Avon. When she's not at her computer, she's traveling, snow skiing, boating, or riding her ATV, dreaming up new stories.

To learn more about Elle James and her stories visit her website at http://www.ellejames.com.

To learn more about Myla Jackson visit her websites at www.mylajackson.com

New York Times & USA Today Bestselling Author

ELLE JAMES

MONTANA
SEAL

BROTHERHOOD PROTECTORS

MONTANA SEAL

BROTHERHOOD PROTECTORS

BOOK #1

ELLE JAMES

New York Times & USA Today
Bestselling Author

Chapter One

"MONTANA, TAKE POINT," Big Bird said. "You'll need to move in fast, once I take out the guard."

Hank Patterson, aka Montana, adjusted his night vision goggles, gripped his M4A1 rifle with the SOP Mod upgrade and rose from his concealed position on the edge of the Iraqi village. U.S. Army intelligence guys had it from a trusted source that an influential leader of the ISIS movement had set up shop in the former home of the now dead Sheik Ghazi Sattar, a paramount chief of the Rishawi tribe. The once palatial estate had taken mortar fire from the Islamic State of Iraq and Syria—or ISIS—rebels. The sheik and his fighters had succumbed to the overpowering forces and died in battle.

In the process, ISIS had gained a stronghold in the village and captured an aid worker the U.S. government wanted returned. When ISIS offered the aid worker in exchange for captured members of their organization, the current administration held to its stand that it didn't negotiate with terrorists.

That's where the Navy SEALs came in. Under the cover of night, armed with limited intel and specialized sound-suppressed weapons,

SEAL Team 10 was to infiltrate the compound, kill the leader, Abu Sayyaf, and liberate the aid worker, who happened to be the Secretary of Defense's niece.

Piece of cake, Montana assured himself. This was what he lived for. Or at least he'd been telling himself that for the past year. He was coming up to the anniversary of his enlistment, and he had to decide whether to get out of the military or re-up. Reenlistment meant more wear and tear on his body and more chances of being shot, blown up or bored out of his mind. When they were called to duty, the missions were intense, yet the downtime gave him too much time to think.

Besides, he wasn't getting any younger. If he didn't leave active duty, he'd end up training SEALs, rather than conducting missions. That would give him even more time to think about what could have been back in his home state.

How many years had it been since he'd visited home? Eight? Ten? Hell, it had been eleven years since he'd been back to Montana for any length of time. One, maybe two days, tops, and he was ready to leave again.

He could remember that defining night like it was yesterday. He'd just broken up with Sadie. He was hurting and wondering if they were insane to give up the best thing that had ever happened to them. Then he and his father had a big blow out. His father called him a lazy, good-for-nothing son and told him to get to work or get out.

Looking back, breaking up with Sadie had

been the best thing, all the way around. She'd gone on to become a Hollywood mega-star, and Montana had gotten the hell away from his father, joined the Navy and become a member of an elite force. Life had turned out pretty good for them both.

So why did he still think about home…and Sadie? Hell, he knew why. Every time his reenlistment came up, he started thinking about home. Most of his friends from high school were married and had children. He'd always wanted kids, but SEALs made crummy parents and spouses. They were gone most of the time, sometimes without a way to contact loved ones back home.

"Be ready." Lieutenant Mike lay next to Montana. "Big Bird, hold your fire until I give the cue."

"Roger," Big Bird responded.

New to the team, Lt. Mike wasn't new to being a SEAL. With four years and ten deployments under his belt, he was a seasoned warrior, although his recent marriage seemed to have slowed him down. He wasn't as quick to leap into a bad situation. And if rumor had it right, his wife was expecting their first child.

"Let's do it," Lt. Mike said.

The muted thump of Big Bird's rifle discharging was Montana's signal to take off.

The ISIS guard who had been pacing the top of a roof slumped forward and fell to the ground with a soft whomp.

3

Montana held his breath, straining his ears for the shout of alarm that didn't come. With the sentry eliminated, Montana had a clear path to the wall. He took off running, hunkered low, his weapon ready, his gaze scanning the top of the wall, searching for the tell-tale green heat signature of a warm body through his night vision goggles.

Swede and Stingray were right behind him.

His skin crawled and his gut clenched. Something didn't feel right. But the mission had to move forward. They had an enemy target to acquire and a woman to rescue before they could go home to Virginia.

Montana knelt at the base of the wall, slung his rifle over his arm, cupped his hands and bent low.

Swede ran up to him, stepped into his cupped hands and launched himself into the air. He hooked his arms over the top, dragged himself over and dropped to the ground below.

Stingray came next, then Nacho, Irish and Lt. Mike.

Big Bird would remain on top of a nearby building and be their eyes and ears for anyone approaching the compound. He'd also provide cover fire for them as they exited with the aid worker.

Lieutenant Mike paused at the top of the wall and reached a hand down to Montana, pulling him up and over.

Swede and Nacho had already moved

forward to the main building, one side of which was caved in, like an open wound. The remaining walls bore pockmarks from bullets and shrapnel. The huge wooden door still stood, closed and strangely unguarded.

"It doesn't feel right," Swede whispered into Montana's headset.

"Stay the course," Lt. Mike responded.

"Going in," Swede acknowledged and slipped into the broken corner of the structure, climbing over the half-wall still standing.

Nacho waited a moment until Swede said, "Clear."

Nacho hopped over the wall and through the crumbled bricks, disappearing into the gaping hole.

Lt. Mike went next, then Montana. Irish brought up the rear.

Once inside, what walls still stood seemed to close in on Montana.

Lt. Mike forged ahead, hurrying past the crumbled bricks and mortar.

Swede and Nacho stood at a door leading deeper into the once ornate residence. Swede wedged a knife into the doorjamb, while Nacho aimed his rifle at the door, ready for anything. A quick jab and the lock gave. Swede nodded to Nacho, yanked open the door and stood back. Nothing happened. Nacho dove through the opening and to the side, leaving room for Swede to follow. Lt. Mike entered next.

The team moved through the building, room

by room.

"There's nobody here," Montana said.

"Then why the guard on top of the building?" Big Bird asked, still connected via the two-way radios in their helmets.

"Suppose it's a trap?" Irish asked.

"We have to check all rooms." Lt. Mike said.

Montana fought a groan. The place had to be over twelve thousand square feet. And that didn't include any underground bunkers that might be a part of the former Sheik's defense plan. Lt. Mike was right. If they didn't check all the rooms, they couldn't say with one hundred percent certainty their ISIS target and the captured aid worker were not there.

Once they'd completed checking the ground floor and upper levels, they started down a set of stairs. These steps weren't finished in the opulent granite tiles of the main level. They were plain concrete, leading to a steel door, heavily reinforced.

Montana took the lead again, fixed C-4 explosives near the handle and pushed a detonator into the clay-like substance.

Everyone backed up the stairs to the main level and held their hands over their ears.

Montana pressed the detonation button. A dull thump shook the floor beneath his feet. A cloud of dust puffed up the staircase.

Lt. Mike held up a hand. "Let it clear a little." Finally, he lowered his hand and led the way back down the stairs to the door.

It hung open on its hinges, a dark, ragged hole blown through the metal. The entrance led to a tunnel-like hallway with doors on either side. Yellowed, florescent lights flickered in the ceiling. Another door marked the end of the long hallway.

The team split, each clearing the rooms, one at a time. None were locked, but the locking mechanisms were on the outsides of the doors. A chill slithered down the back of Montana's neck, partly because of the coolness in the basement and partly from knowing the sheik had probably used the rooms to incarcerate people. Nothing in any of the rooms indicated the aid worker had been imprisoned there.

At the end of the corridor, the final door was locked. Once again, Montana set the charge, the team hid behind the doors of the cell-like rooms, waiting for the charge to blow. Montana only used enough explosive to dislodge the lock mechanism, no more. He didn't want to destroy the structure of the underground portion of the building and risk trapping his team or causing them injury with the concussion.

"You have a gift." Nacho grinned as he passed Montana and followed Lt. Mike into a much narrower tunnel.

"We're in a tunnel beneath the compound," Lt. Mike said into the two-way radio.

Montana doubted Big Bird would hear on the outside. Where the tunnel would lead, they'd know soon enough. Unfortunately, they wouldn't have a sniper on the other end providing cover for them when they emerged from whatever building.

His gut twisting, his nerves stretched, Montana clenched his weapon, holding it at the ready as he continued forward. If they had any chance of rescuing the aid worker, it had to be soon. ISIS rebels had a habit of torturing and killing anyone they could use as an example, rather than hanging on to them. Prisoners only slowed the attack and hampered their determination to take everything in their paths.

The tunnel opened into the bowels of what appeared to be a warehouse.

"I feel like we're on a wild goose chase," Swede muttered.

"And the goose is leading us to the slaughter. Not the other way around," Irish concurred.

They climbed a set of stairs to a huge, empty room.

"Damn," Swede said and bent to a dark lump on the ground.

Nacho released a string of profanity in Spanish.

"We've found the aid worker."

What Montana had assumed was a pile of rags, was in fact a woman, her clothes torn, her body ravaged, her face battered. Her eyes were wide open, staring up at the ceiling.

Swede knelt beside her and touched his fingers to the base of her throat.

Montana's stomach roiled at the sight of the woman's damaged body. He could have told

Swede she was already dead. What a waste of life. And for what? "We need to get out of here."

The sound of footsteps made Montana glance up. A man stood on a catwalk twenty feet above them. He shouted something in Pashtu, ending in *Allah*, pulled the pin on a grenade and tossed it into the middle of the team.

"Fuck!" Montana yanked his weapon around and shot the man. He fell to the ground, but killing him was a little too late.

The grenade rolled toward Swede, still crouched beside the woman's body.

"Get down!" Lt. Mike shouted, and then threw himself over the grenade.

Montana shouted, "No!" as the grenade exploded beneath their leader.

The force of the concussion reverberated throughout the room, knocking Montana to the ground. His last thoughts were of the home and the girl he'd once loved

Also by Elle James